For Better or For Worse:

It All Comes Out in the Wash

Lynn
Johnston

TOR

A TOM DOHERTY ASSOCIATES BOOK
NEW YORK

FOR BETTER OR FOR WORSE: IT ALL COMES OUT IN THE WASH

A TOR Book
Published by Tom Doherty Associates, Inc.
49 West 24 Street
New York, NY 10010

ISBN: 0-812-50692-8 Can. ISBN: 0-812-50693-6

First Tor edition: March 1990

Printed in the United States of America

0 9 8 7 6 5 4 3 2 1

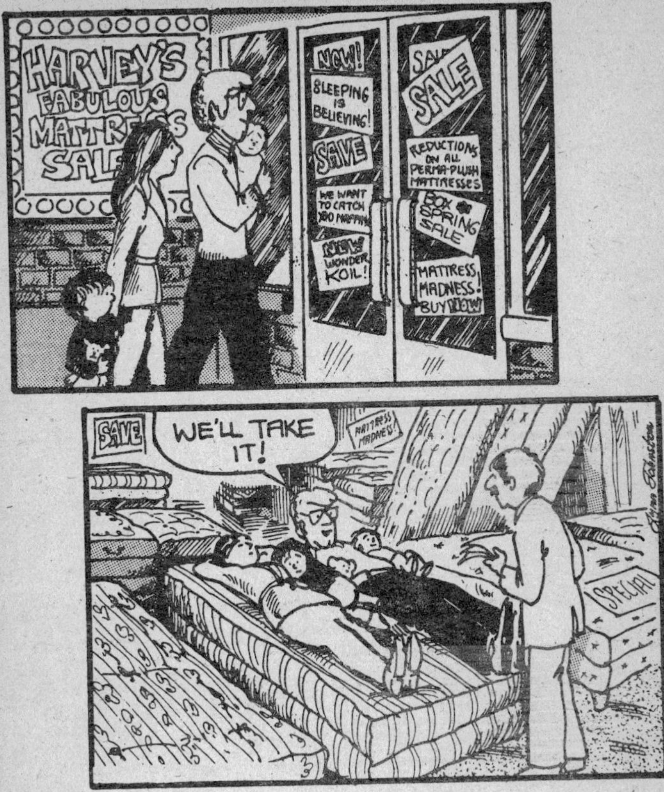
HARVEY'S
FABULOUS
NEW!
SLEEPING IS BELIEVING!
SAVE
WE WANT TO CATCH
NEW WONDER KOIL!
SALE
REDUCTIONS ON ALL PERMA-PLUSH MATTRESSES
BOX SPRING SALE
MATTRESS MADNESS! BUY NOW!
SAVE
WE'LL TAKE IT!
MATTRESS MADNESS!
SPECIAL

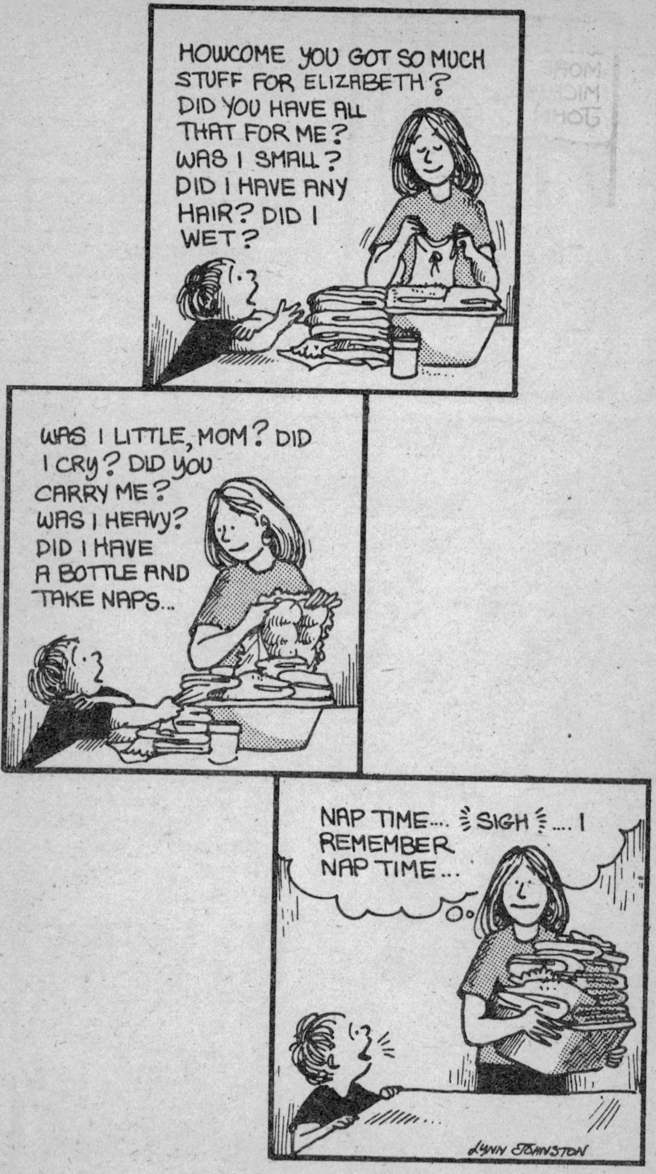
HOWCOME YOU GOT SO MUCH STUFF FOR ELIZABETH? DID YOU HAVE ALL THAT FOR ME? WAS I SMALL? DID I HAVE ANY HAIR? DID I WET?
WAS I LITTLE, MOM? DID I CRY? DID YOU CARRY ME? WAS I HEAVY? DID I HAVE A BOTTLE AND TAKE NAPS...
NAP TIME.... SIGH .... I REMEMBER NAP TIME...
LYNN JOHNSTON

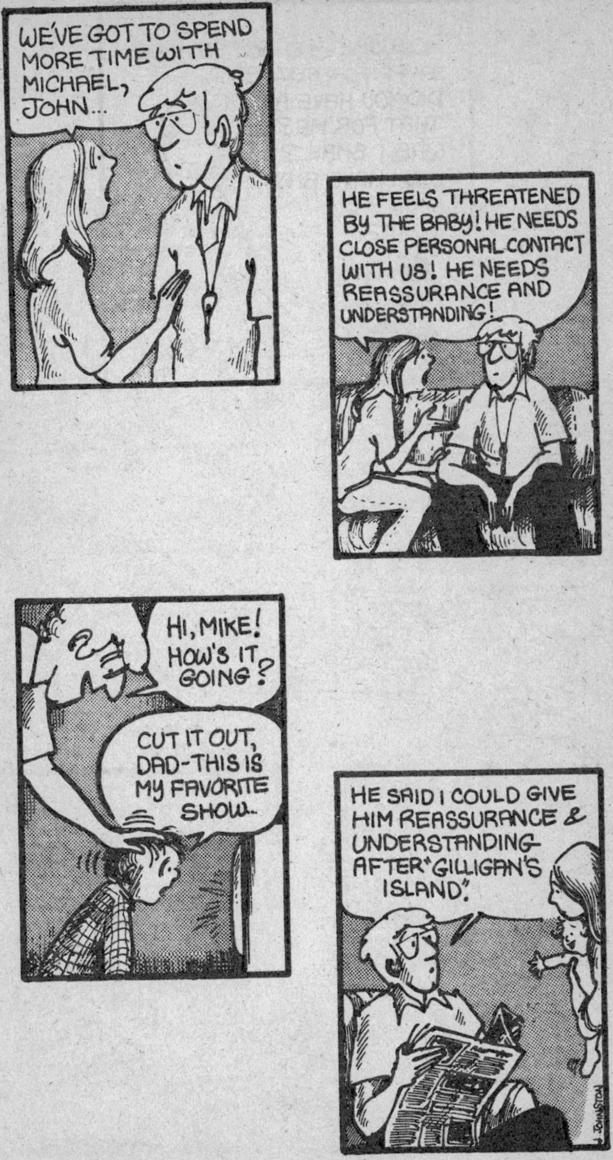
WE'VE GOT TO SPEND MORE TIME WITH MICHAEL, JOHN...
HE FEELS THREATENED BY THE BABY! HE NEEDS CLOSE PERSONAL CONTACT WITH US! HE NEEDS REASSURANCE AND UNDERSTANDING!
HI, MIKE! HOW'S IT GOING?
CUT IT OUT, DAD-THIS IS MY FAVORITE SHOW..
HE SAID I COULD GIVE HIM REASSURANCE & UNDERSTANDING AFTER "GILLIGAN'S ISLAND".
J. JOHNSTON

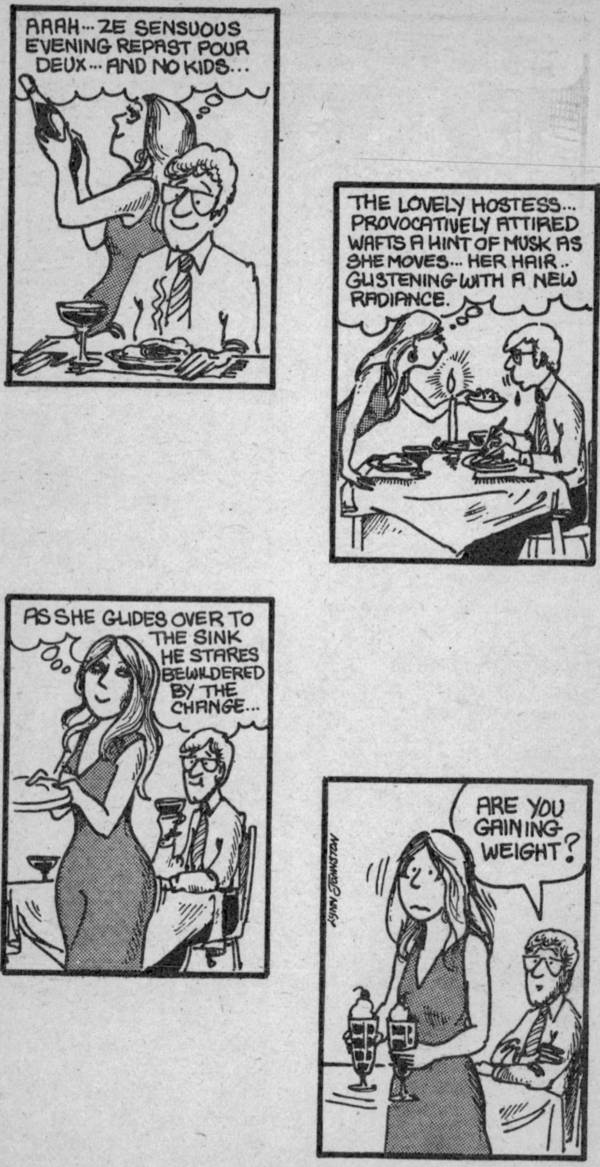
ARRH... ZE SENSUOUS EVENING REPAST POUR DEUX... AND NO KIDS...
THE LOVELY HOSTESS... PROVOCATIVELY ATTIRED WAFTS A HINT OF MUSK AS SHE MOVES... HER HAIR.. GLISTENING WITH A NEW RADIANCE.
AS SHE GLIDES OVER TO THE SINK HE STARES BEWILDERED BY THE CHANGE...
LYNN JOHNSTON
ARE YOU GAINING WEIGHT?

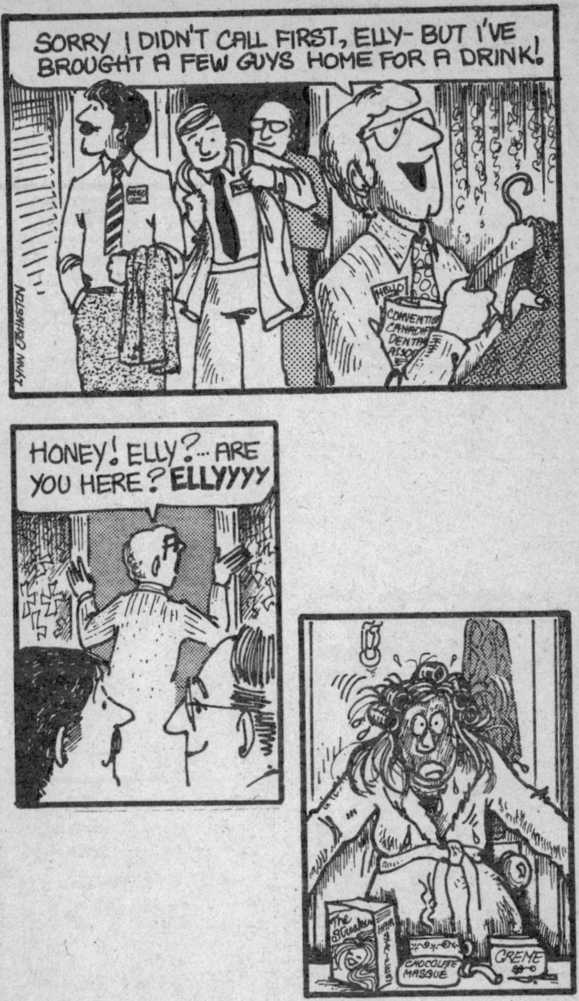
SORRY I DIDN'T CALL FIRST, ELLY- BUT I'VE BROUGHT A FEW GUYS HOME FOR A DRINK!
LYNN JOHNSTON
HELLO
HONEY! ELLY?... ARE YOU HERE? ELLYYYY
CHOCOLATE MASQUE
CREME

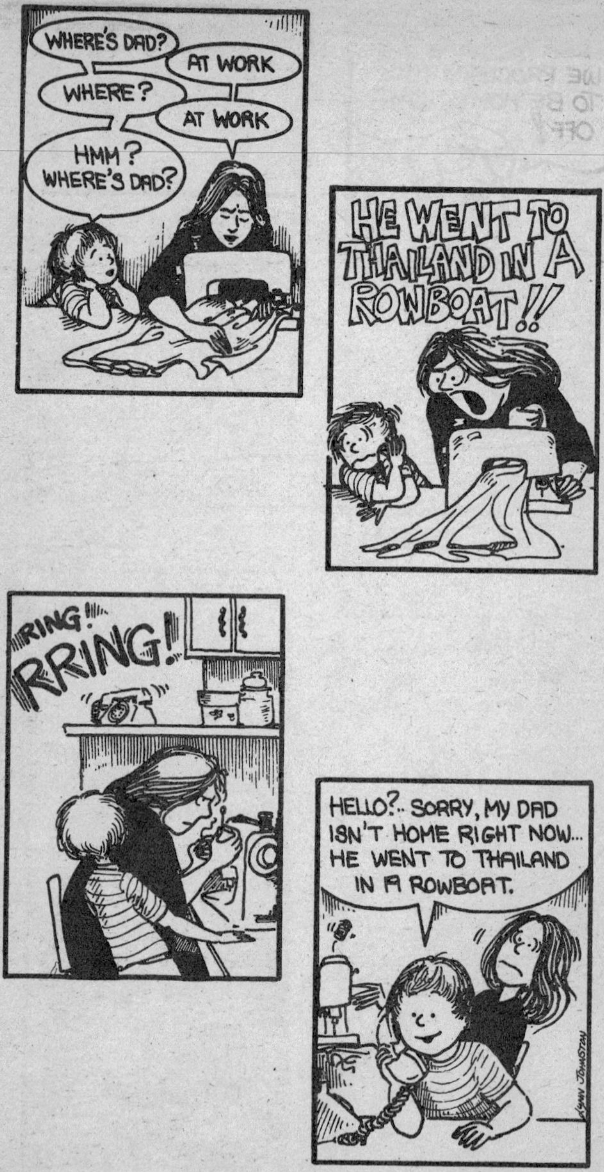
WHERE'S DAD?
AT WORK
WHERE?
AT WORK
HMM? WHERE'S DAD?
HE WENT TO THAILAND IN A ROWBOAT!!
RING!
RRING!
HELLO?.. SORRY, MY DAD ISN'T HOME RIGHT NOW... HE WENT TO THAILAND IN A ROWBOAT.
LYNN JOHNSTON

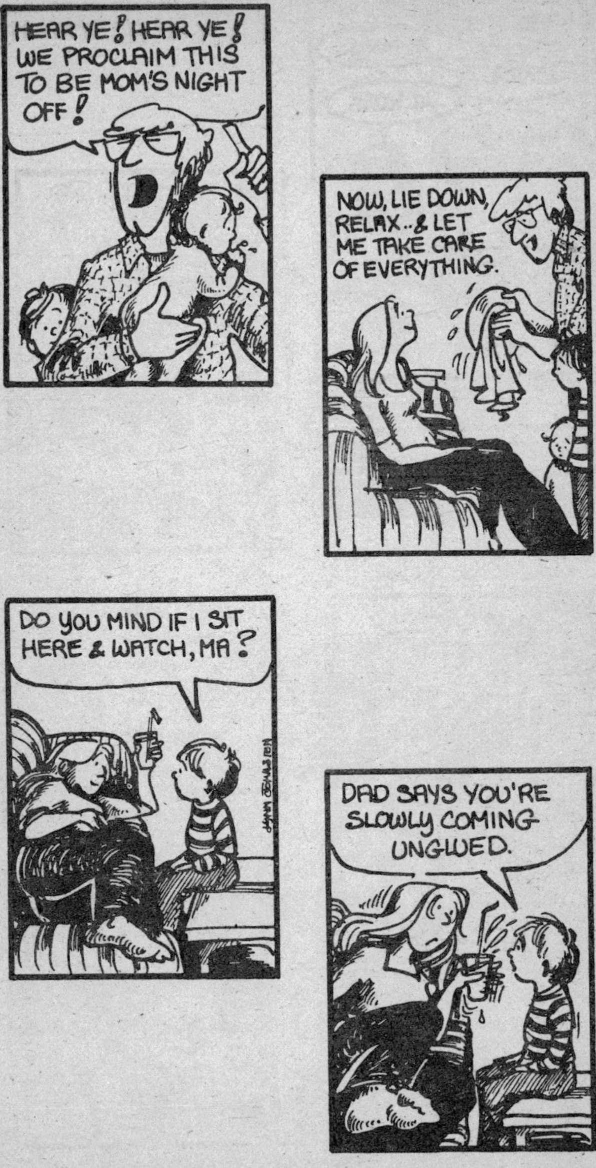
HEAR YE! HEAR YE! WE PROCLAIM THIS TO BE MOM'S NIGHT OFF!
NOW, LIE DOWN, RELAX...& LET ME TAKE CARE OF EVERYTHING.
DO YOU MIND IF I SIT HERE & WATCH, MA?
DAD SAYS YOU'RE SLOWLY COMING UNGLUED.

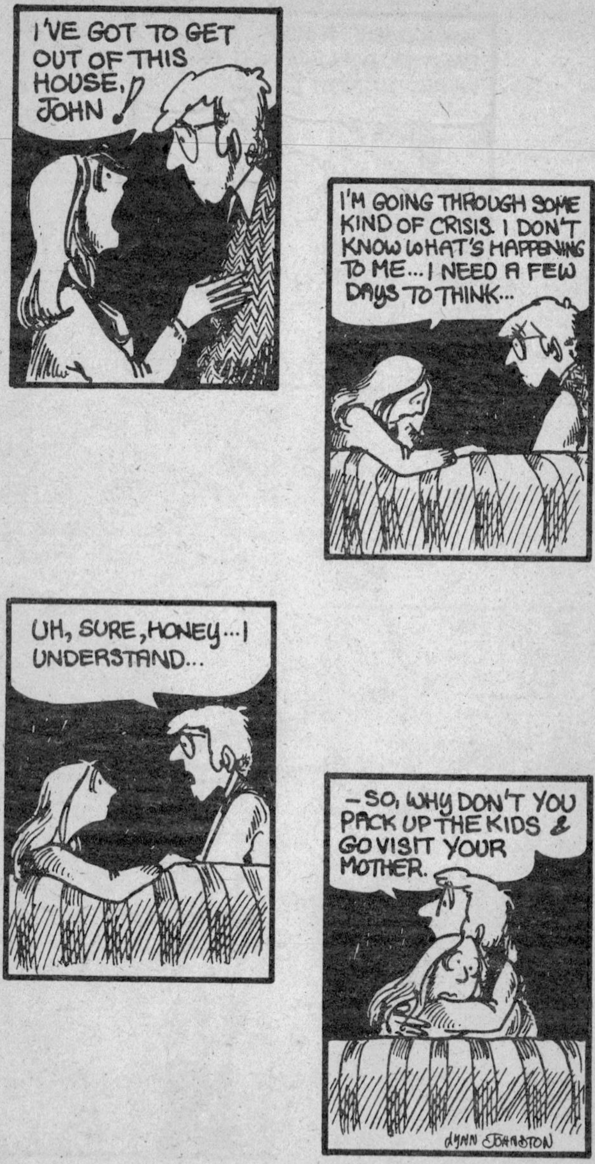
I'VE GOT TO GET OUT OF THIS HOUSE, JOHN!
I'M GOING THROUGH SOME KIND OF CRISIS. I DON'T KNOW WHAT'S HAPPENING TO ME... I NEED A FEW DAYS TO THINK...
UH, SURE, HONEY... I UNDERSTAND...
—SO, WHY DON'T YOU PACK UP THE KIDS & GO VISIT YOUR MOTHER.
LYNN JOHNSTON

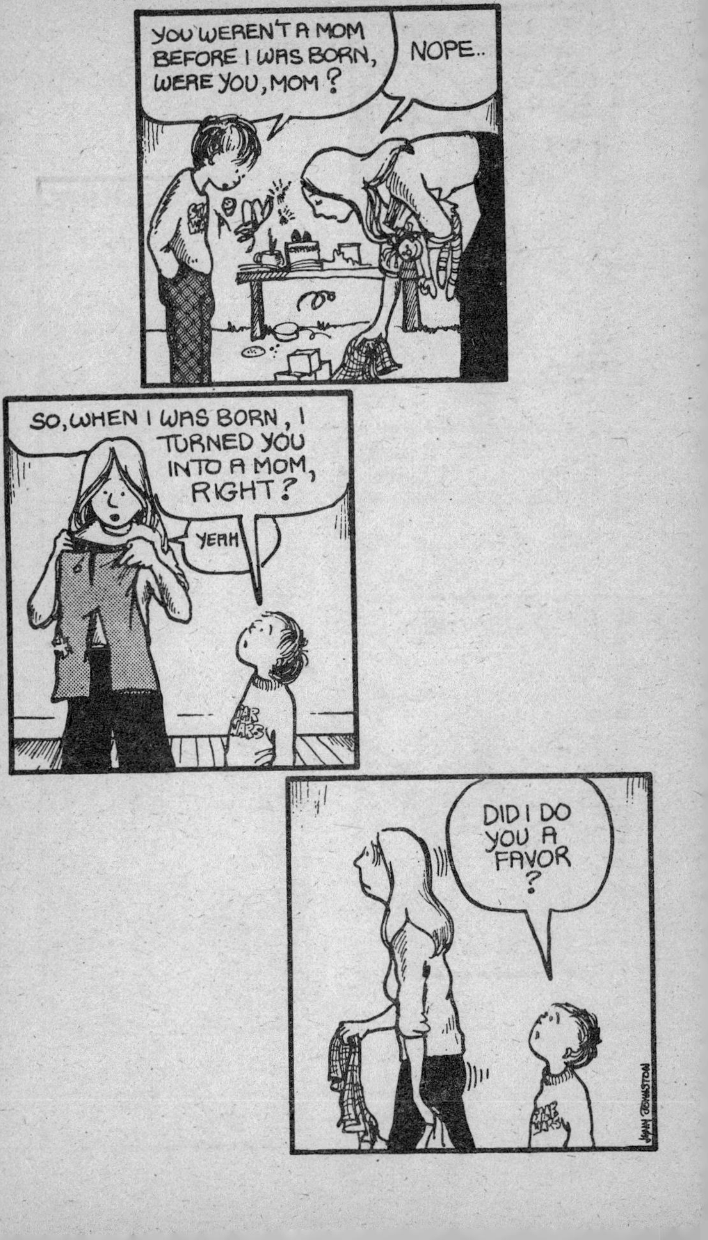
YOU WEREN'T A MOM BEFORE I WAS BORN, WERE YOU, MOM?
NOPE..
SO, WHEN I WAS BORN, I TURNED YOU INTO A MOM, RIGHT?
YEAH
DID I DO YOU A FAVOR?
LYNN JOHNSTON

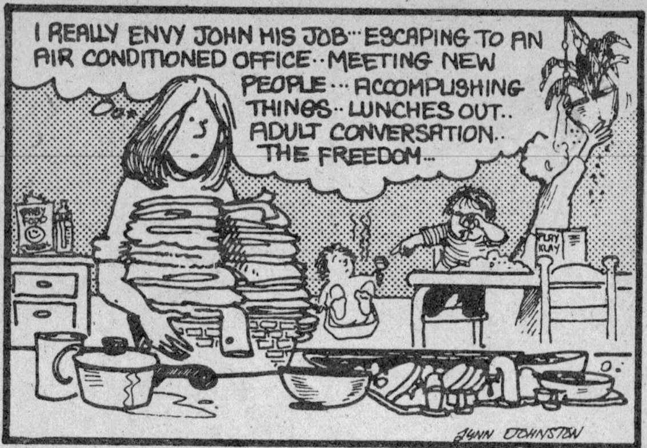
I REALLY ENVY JOHN HIS JOB... ESCAPING TO AN AIR CONDITIONED OFFICE.. MEETING NEW PEOPLE... ACCOMPLISHING THINGS.. LUNCHES OUT.. ADULT CONVERSATION.. THE FREEDOM...
PLAY KLAY
LYNN JOHNSTON

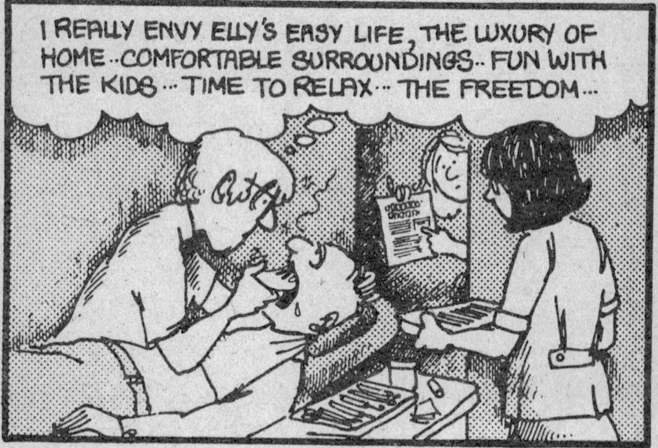
I REALLY ENVY ELLY'S EASY LIFE, THE LUXURY OF HOME..COMFORTABLE SURROUNDINGS.. FUN WITH THE KIDS... TIME TO RELAX... THE FREEDOM...

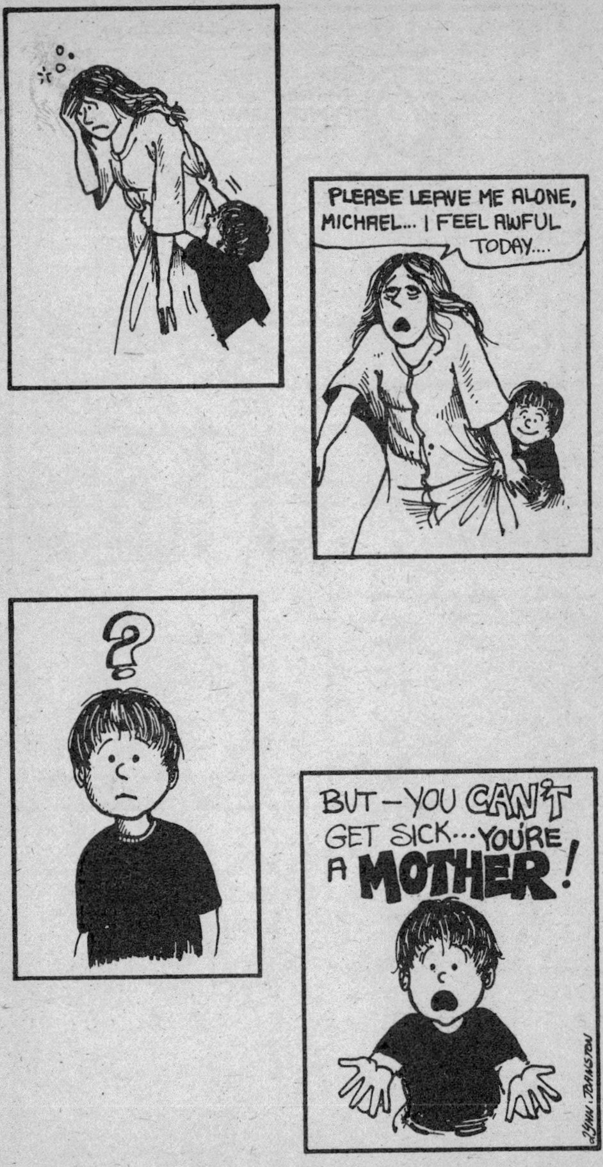
PLEASE LEAVE ME ALONE, MICHAEL... I FEEL AWFUL TODAY....
?
BUT—YOU CAN'T GET SICK... YOU'RE A MOTHER!
LYNN JOHNSTON

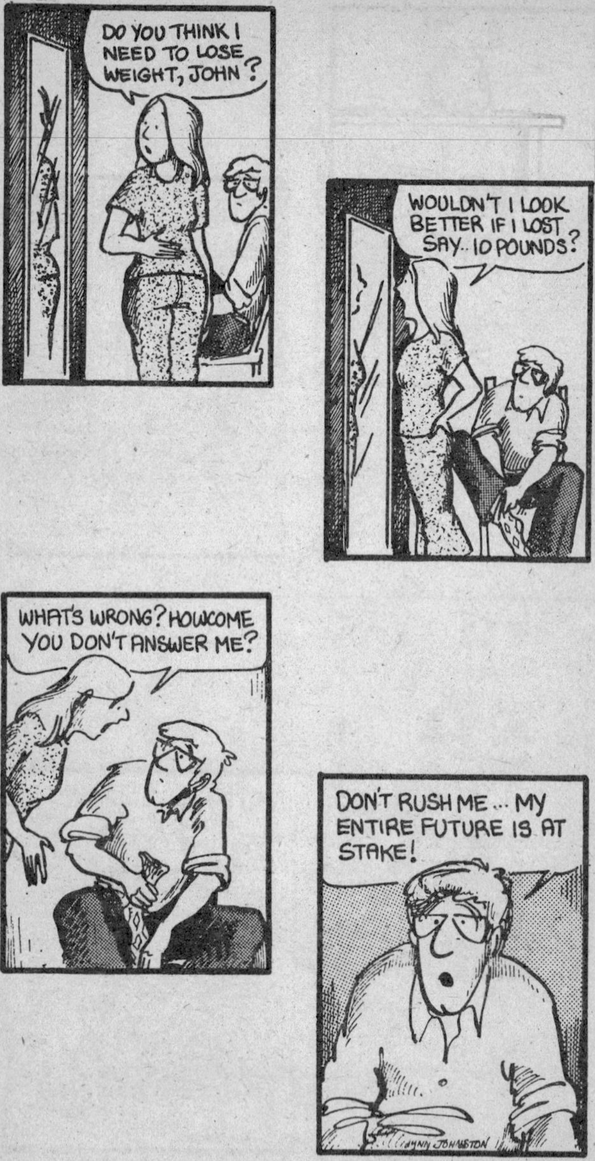
DO YOU THINK I NEED TO LOSE WEIGHT, JOHN?
WOULDN'T I LOOK BETTER IF I LOST SAY.. 10 POUNDS?
WHAT'S WRONG? HOWCOME YOU DON'T ANSWER ME?
DON'T RUSH ME... MY ENTIRE FUTURE IS AT STAKE!
LYNN JOHNSTON

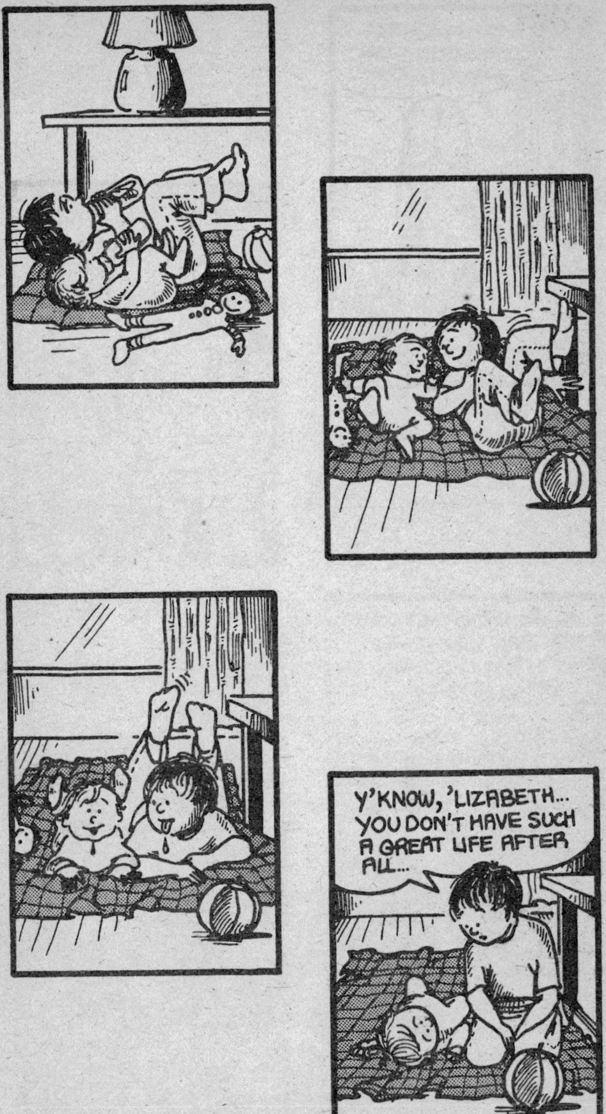
Y'KNOW, 'LIZABETH... YOU DON'T HAVE SUCH A GREAT LIFE AFTER ALL...
Lynn Johnston

YOU'RE GOING TO KINDERGARTEN - & STOP THAT PHONEY SICK ROUTINE!
RRINGGG
MRS PATTERSON, WE'RE SENDING MICHAEL HOME. HE'S RUNNING A FEVER & IS MUCH TOO ILL TO BE OUT.
THEY NEVER ACTUALLY COME OUT AND CALL YOU NEGLIGENT...
LYNN JOHNSTON

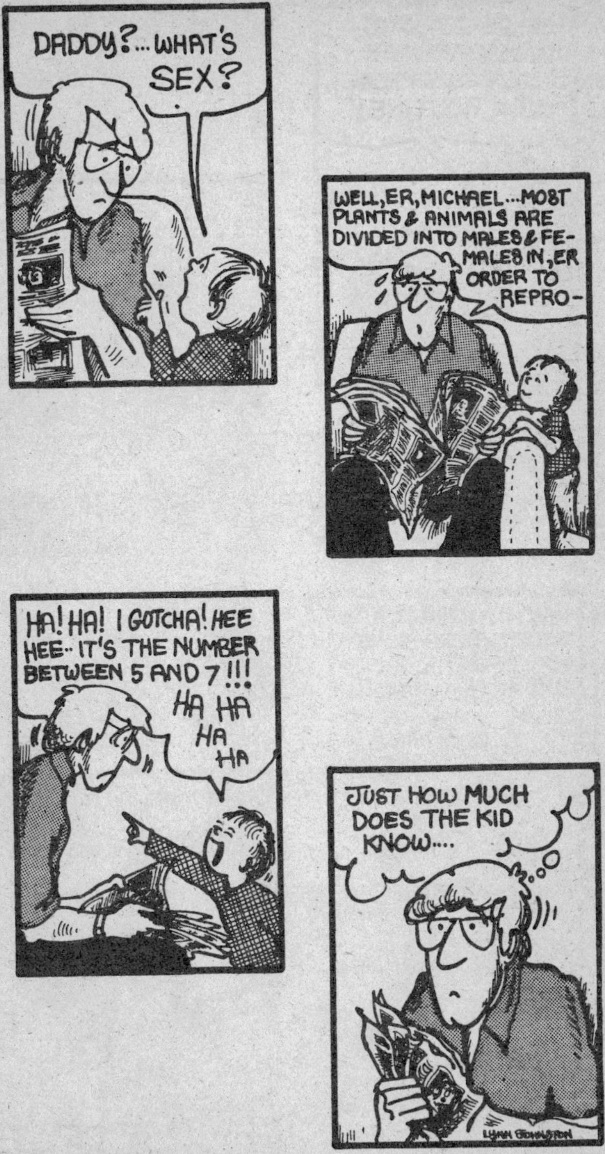
DADDY?... WHAT'S SEX?
WELL, ER, MICHAEL... MOST PLANTS & ANIMALS ARE DIVIDED INTO MALES & FE-MALES IN, ER ORDER TO REPRO-
HA! HA! I GOTCHA! HEE HEE.. IT'S THE NUMBER BETWEEN 5 AND 7!!! HA HA HA HA
JUST HOW MUCH DOES THE KID KNOW....
LYNN JOHNSTON

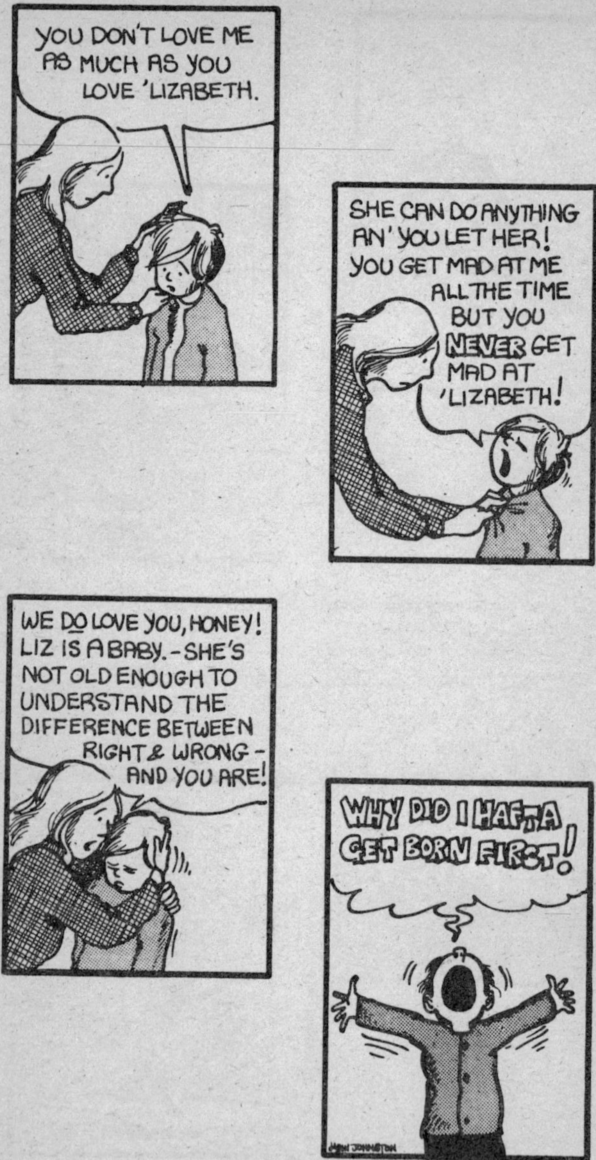
YOU DON'T LOVE ME AS MUCH AS YOU LOVE 'LIZABETH.
SHE CAN DO ANYTHING AN' YOU LET HER! YOU GET MAD AT ME ALL THE TIME BUT YOU NEVER GET MAD AT 'LIZABETH!
WE DO LOVE YOU, HONEY! LIZ IS A BABY. - SHE'S NOT OLD ENOUGH TO UNDERSTAND THE DIFFERENCE BETWEEN RIGHT & WRONG - AND YOU ARE!
WHY DID I HAFTA GET BORN FIRST!

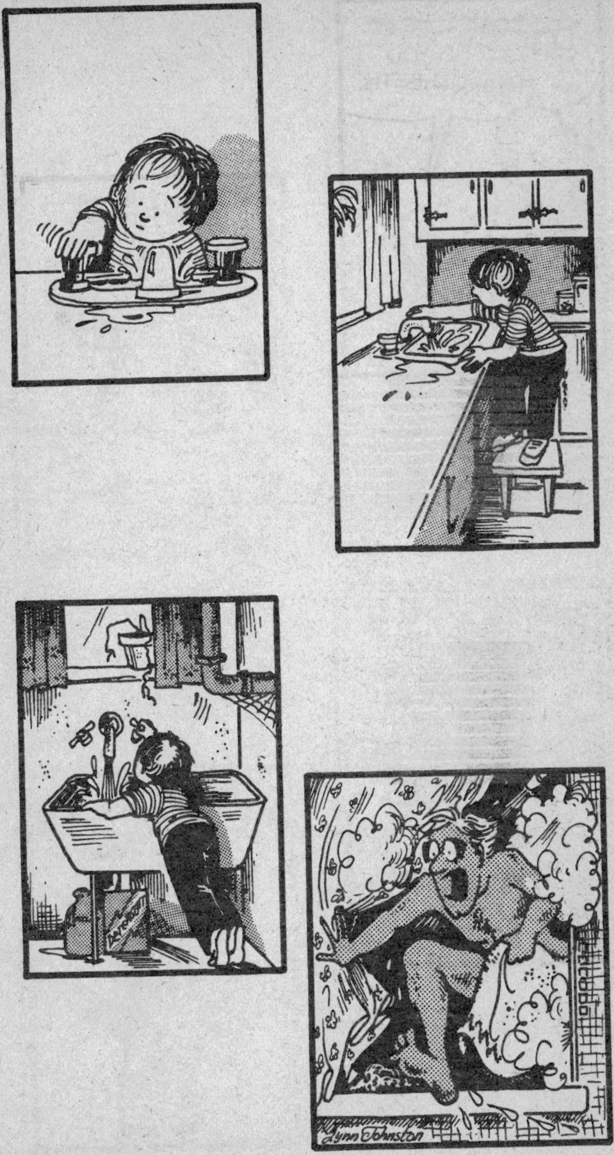
Lynn Johnston

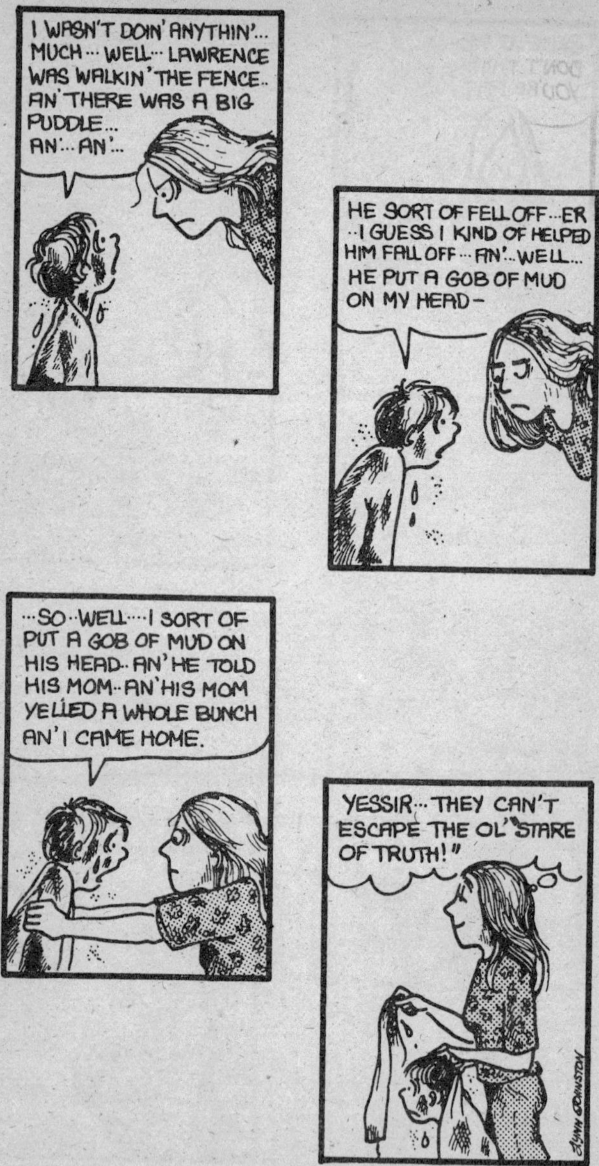
I WASN'T DOIN' ANYTHIN'... MUCH ... WELL... LAWRENCE WAS WALKIN' THE FENCE.. AN' THERE WAS A BIG PUDDLE... AN'... AN'...
HE SORT OF FELL OFF...ER ..I GUESS I KIND OF HELPED HIM FALL OFF ... AN'...WELL... HE PUT A GOB OF MUD ON MY HEAD-
...SO..WELL....I SORT OF PUT A GOB OF MUD ON HIS HEAD.. AN' HE TOLD HIS MOM..AN' HIS MOM YELLED A WHOLE BUNCH AN' I CAME HOME.
YESSIR... THEY CAN'T ESCAPE THE OL' "STARE OF TRUTH!"
LYNN JOHNSTON

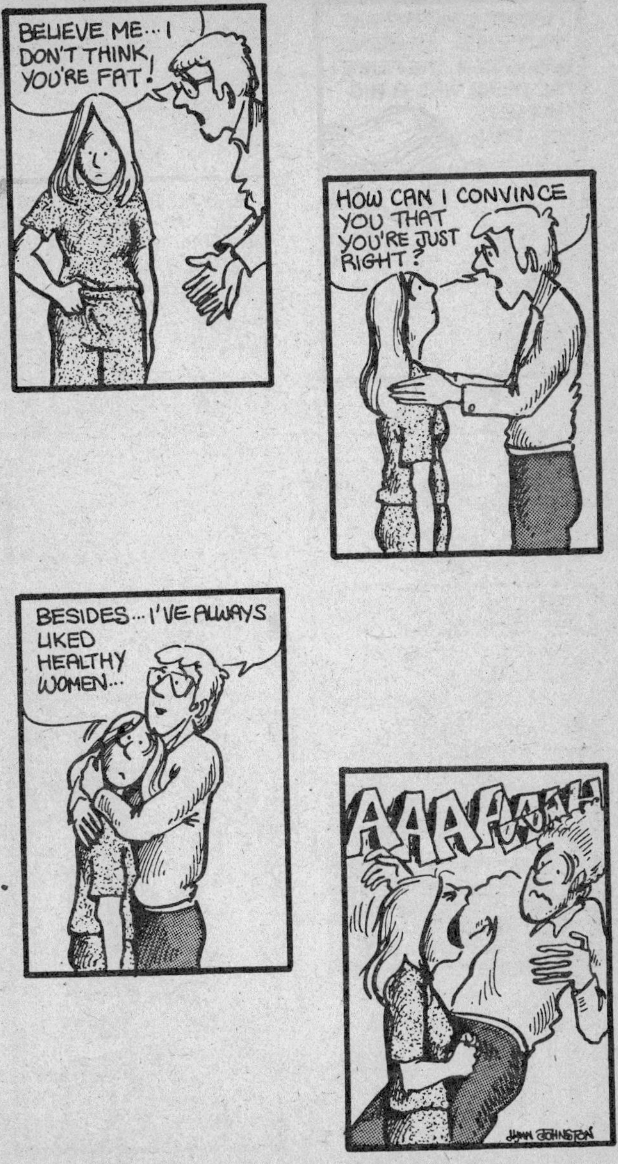
BELIEVE ME... I DON'T THINK YOU'RE FAT!
HOW CAN I CONVINCE YOU THAT YOU'RE JUST RIGHT?
BESIDES... I'VE ALWAYS LIKED HEALTHY WOMEN...
AAAAGH
LYNN JOHNSTON

UGH!
HISS
MEEEOW!
SCRATCH
PFFTT!
OW!
PUFF
PUFF
PUFF
THIS KITTY FOLLOWED ME HOME, MA... CAN WE KEEP HIM?

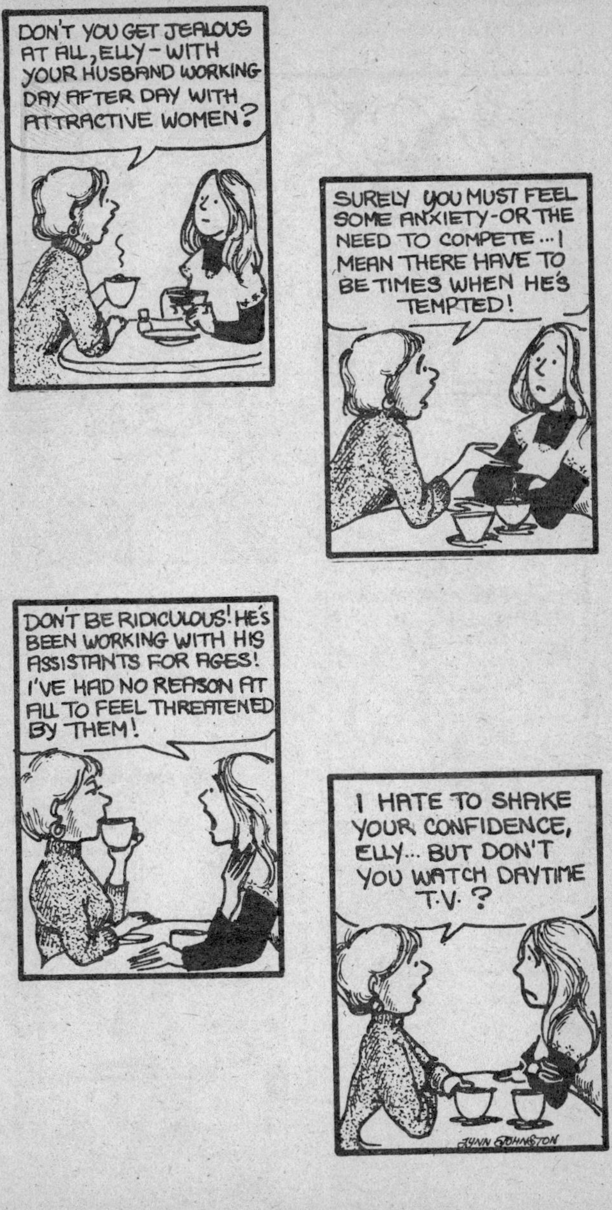
DON'T YOU GET JEALOUS AT ALL, ELLY - WITH YOUR HUSBAND WORKING DAY AFTER DAY WITH ATTRACTIVE WOMEN?
SURELY YOU MUST FEEL SOME ANXIETY - OR THE NEED TO COMPETE... I MEAN THERE HAVE TO BE TIMES WHEN HE'S TEMPTED!
DON'T BE RIDICULOUS! HE'S BEEN WORKING WITH HIS ASSISTANTS FOR AGES! I'VE HAD NO REASON AT ALL TO FEEL THREATENED BY THEM!
I HATE TO SHAKE YOUR CONFIDENCE, ELLY... BUT DON'T YOU WATCH DAYTIME T.V.?
LYNN JOHNSTON

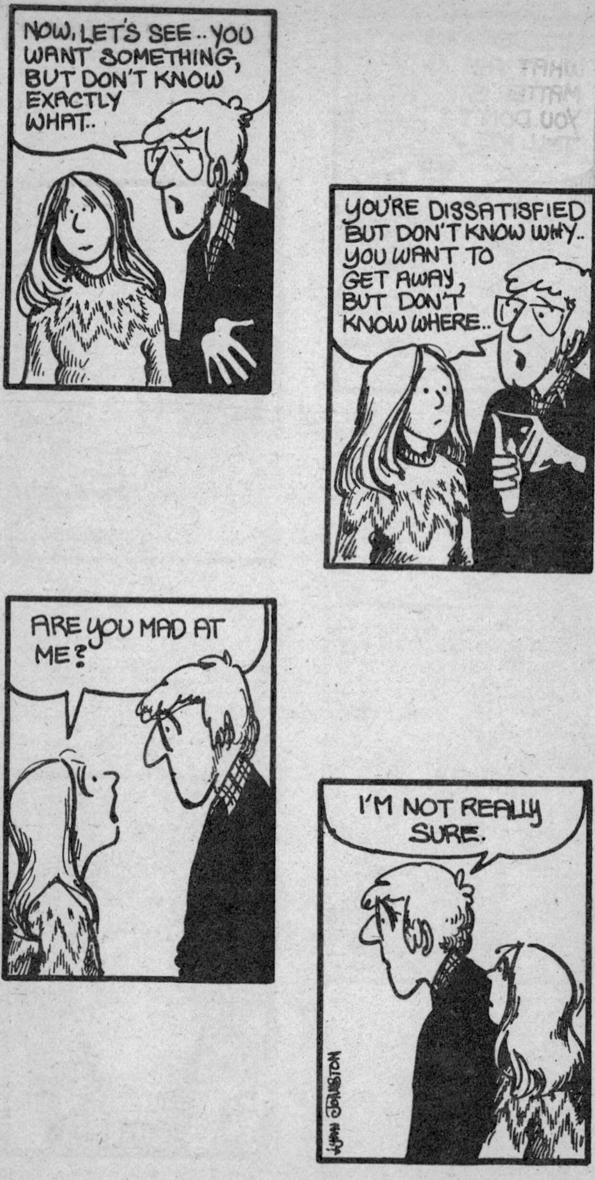
NOW, LET'S SEE .. YOU WANT SOMETHING, BUT DON'T KNOW EXACTLY WHAT..
YOU'RE DISSATISFIED BUT DON'T KNOW WHY.. YOU WANT TO GET AWAY, BUT DON'T KNOW WHERE..
ARE YOU MAD AT ME?
I'M NOT REALLY SURE.
LYNN JOHNSTON

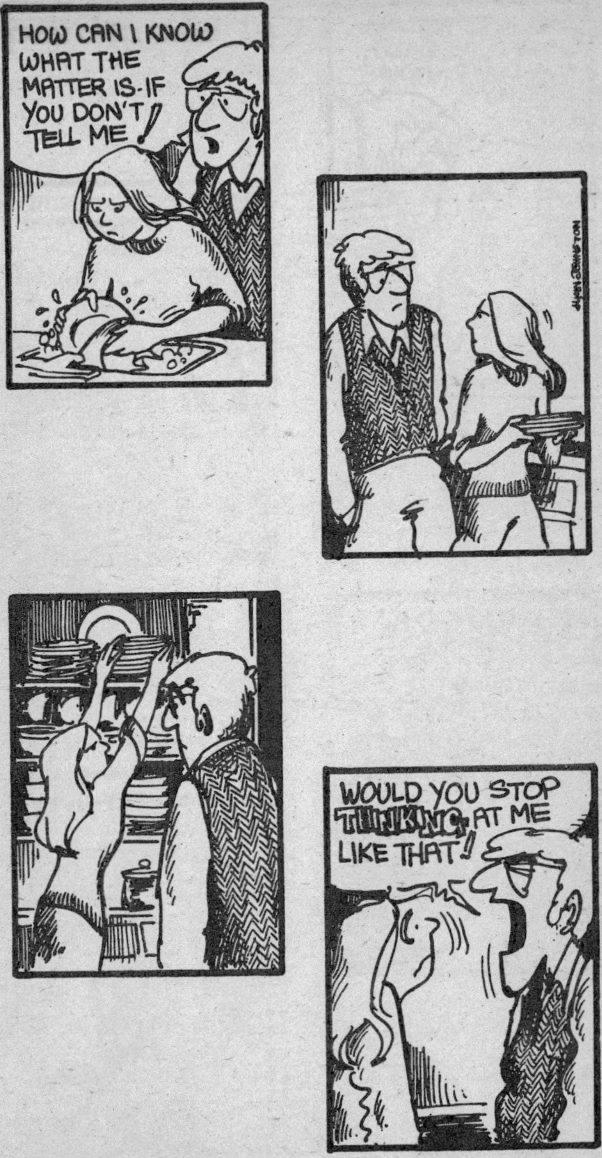
HOW CAN I KNOW WHAT THE MATTER IS-IF YOU DON'T TELL ME!
LYNN JOHNSTON
WOULD YOU STOP THINKING AT ME LIKE THAT!

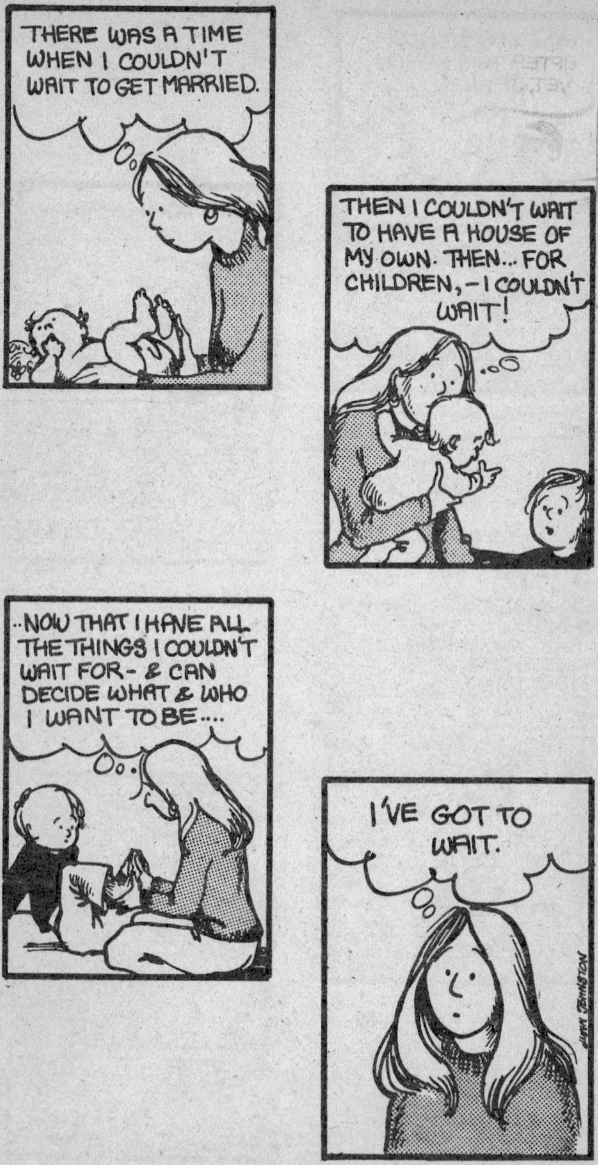
THERE WAS A TIME WHEN I COULDN'T WAIT TO GET MARRIED.
THEN I COULDN'T WAIT TO HAVE A HOUSE OF MY OWN. THEN... FOR CHILDREN, – I COULDN'T WAIT!
..NOW THAT I HAVE ALL THE THINGS I COULDN'T WAIT FOR – & CAN DECIDE WHAT & WHO I WANT TO BE....
I'VE GOT TO WAIT.

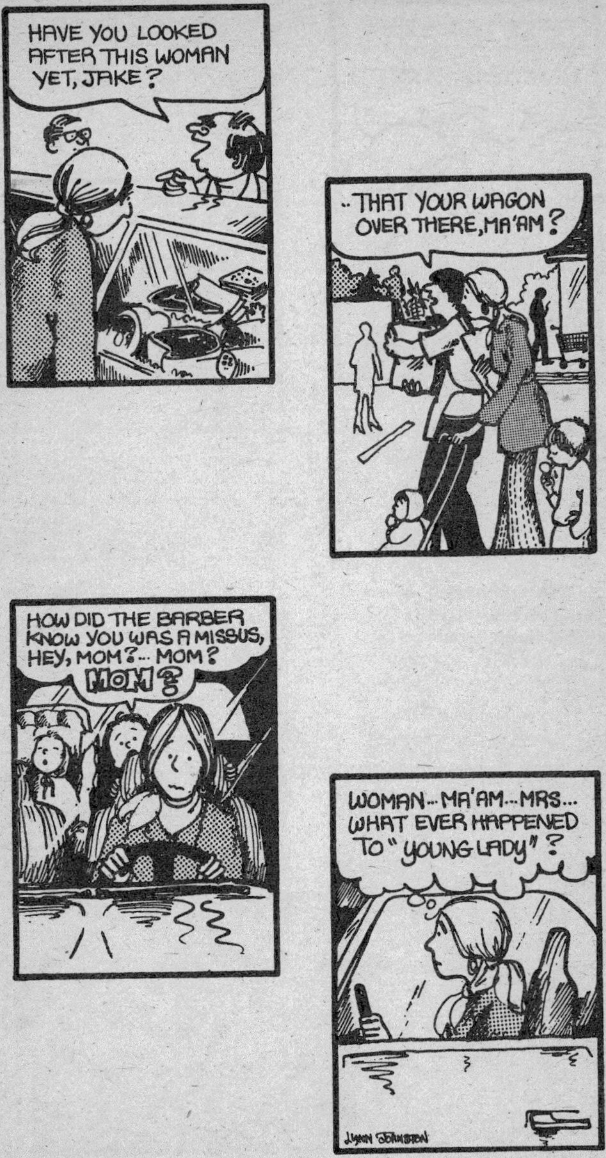
HAVE YOU LOOKED AFTER THIS WOMAN YET, JAKE?
..THAT YOUR WAGON OVER THERE, MA'AM?
HOW DID THE BARBER KNOW YOU WAS A MISSUS, HEY, MOM?... MOM? MOM?
WOMAN... MA'AM... MRS... WHAT EVER HAPPENED TO "YOUNG LADY"?
LYNN JOHNSTON

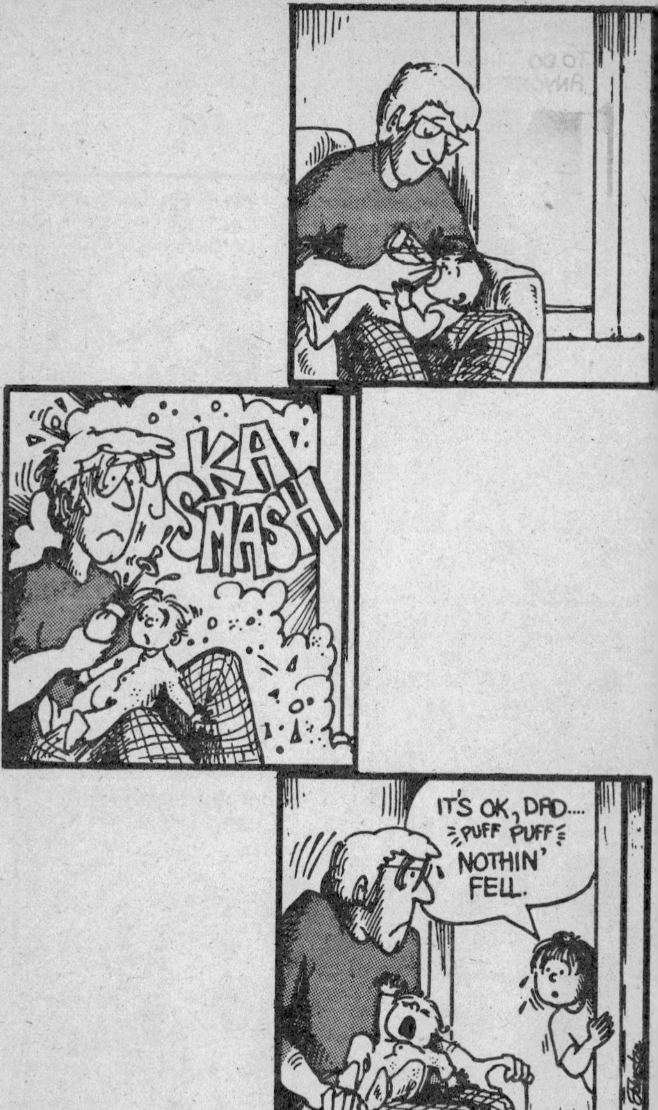
KA SMASH
IT'S OK, DAD....
PUFF PUFF
NOTHIN' FELL.

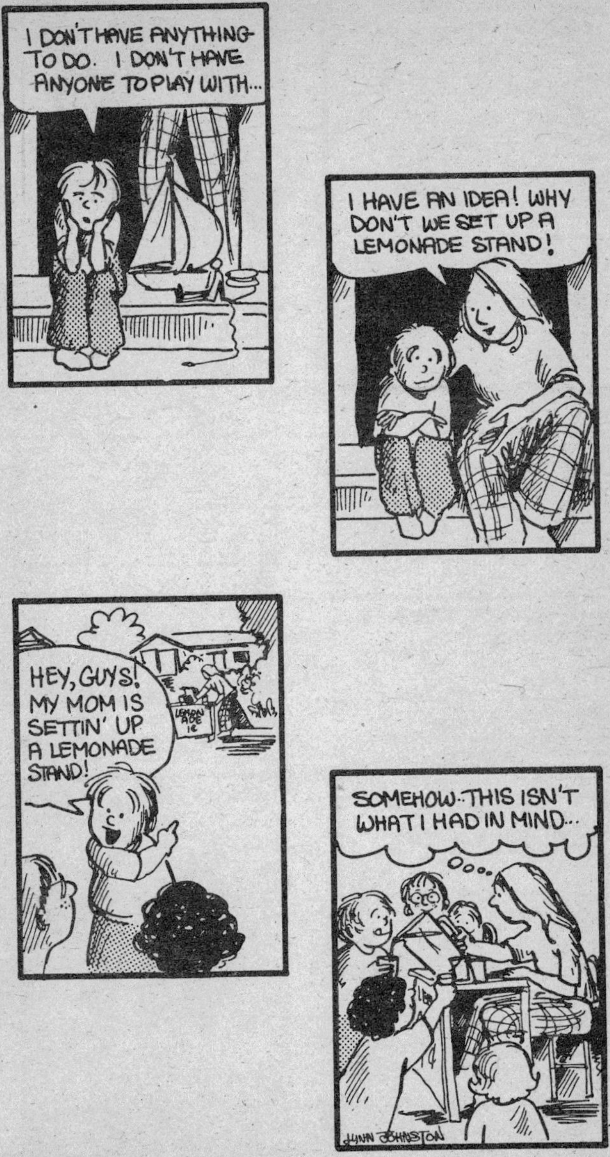
I DON'T HAVE ANYTHING TO DO. I DON'T HAVE ANYONE TO PLAY WITH...
I HAVE AN IDEA! WHY DON'T WE SET UP A LEMONADE STAND!
HEY, GUYS! MY MOM IS SETTIN' UP A LEMONADE STAND!
SOMEHOW.. THIS ISN'T WHAT I HAD IN MIND...
LYNN JOHNSTON

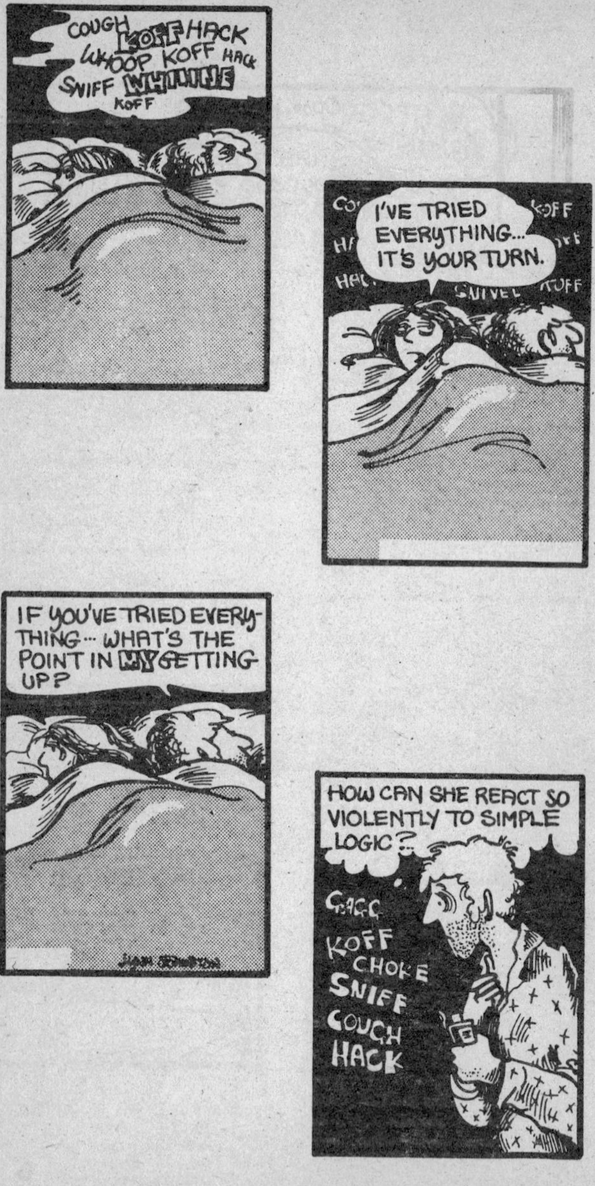
COUGH KOFF HACK
WHOOP KOFF HACK
SNIFF WHINE
KOFF
I'VE TRIED EVERYTHING... IT'S YOUR TURN.
IF YOU'VE TRIED EVERYTHING... WHAT'S THE POINT IN MY GETTING UP?
HOW CAN SHE REACT SO VIOLENTLY TO SIMPLE LOGIC?..
GAGG
KOFF
CHOKE
SNIFF
COUGH
HACK

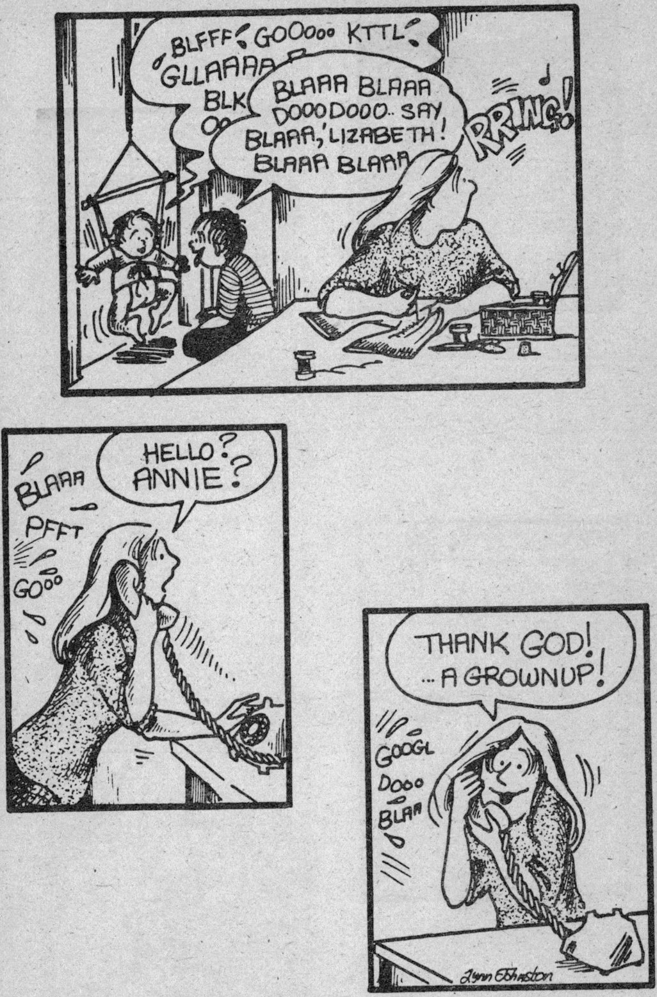
BLFFF! GOOooo KTTL! GLLAAAA BLK Oo
BLAAA BLAAA DOOODOOO.. SAY, BLAAA, 'LIZABETH! BLAAA BLAAA
RRING!
BLAAA PFFT GOoo
HELLO? ANNIE?
GOOGL DOOO BLAA
THANK GOD! ...A GROWNUP!
Lynn Johnston

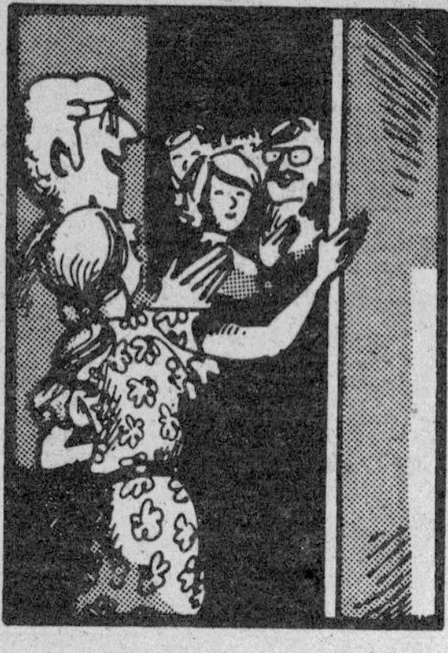

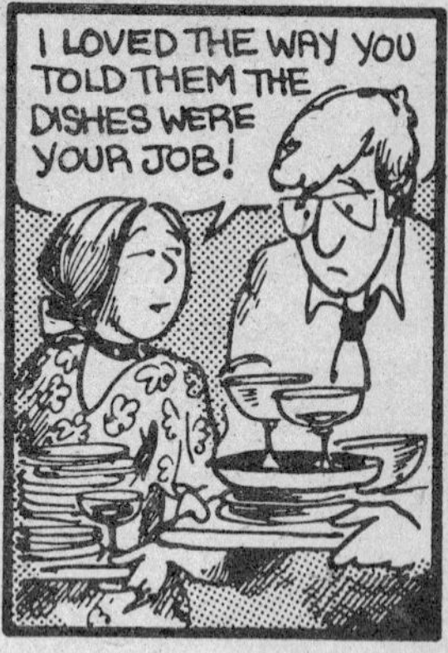
I LOVED THE WAY YOU TOLD THEM THE DISHES WERE YOUR JOB!

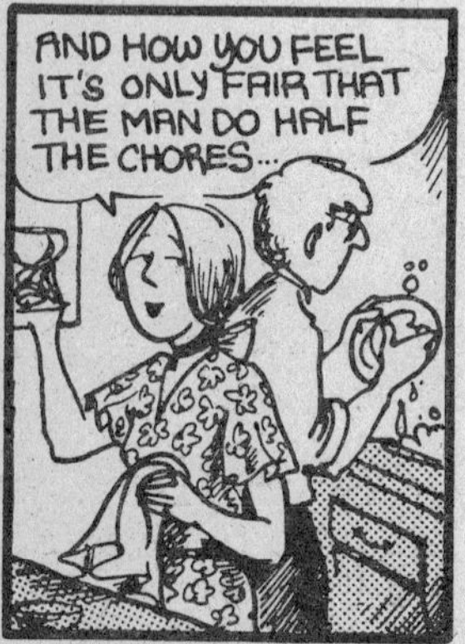
AND HOW YOU FEEL IT'S ONLY FAIR THAT THE MAN DO HALF THE CHORES...

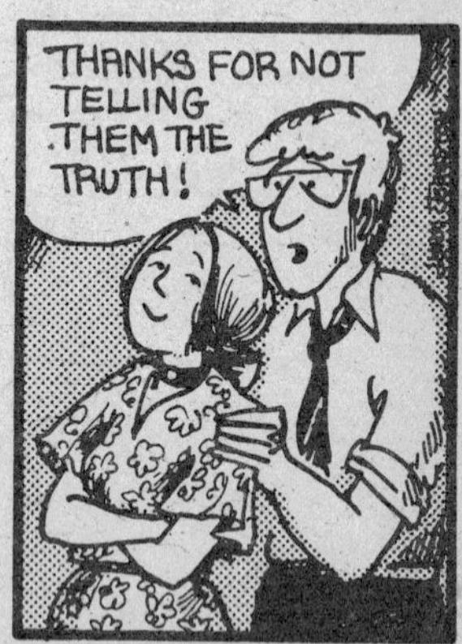
THANKS FOR NOT TELLING THEM THE TRUTH!

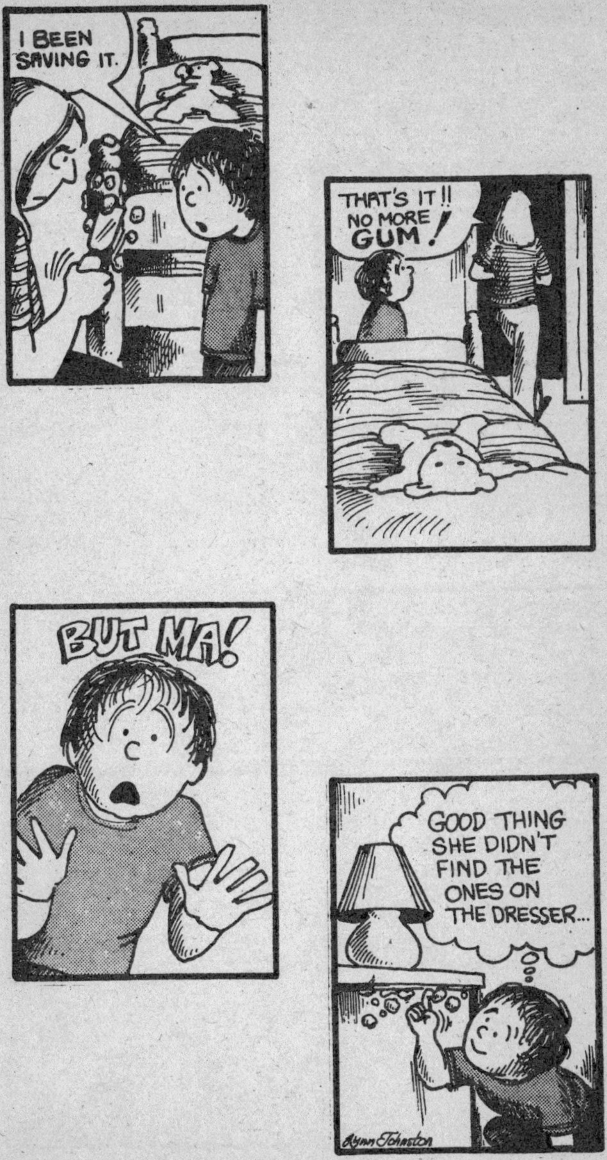
I BEEN SAVING IT.
THAT'S IT!! NO MORE GUM!
BUT MA!
GOOD THING SHE DIDN'T FIND THE ONES ON THE DRESSER...
Lynn Johnston

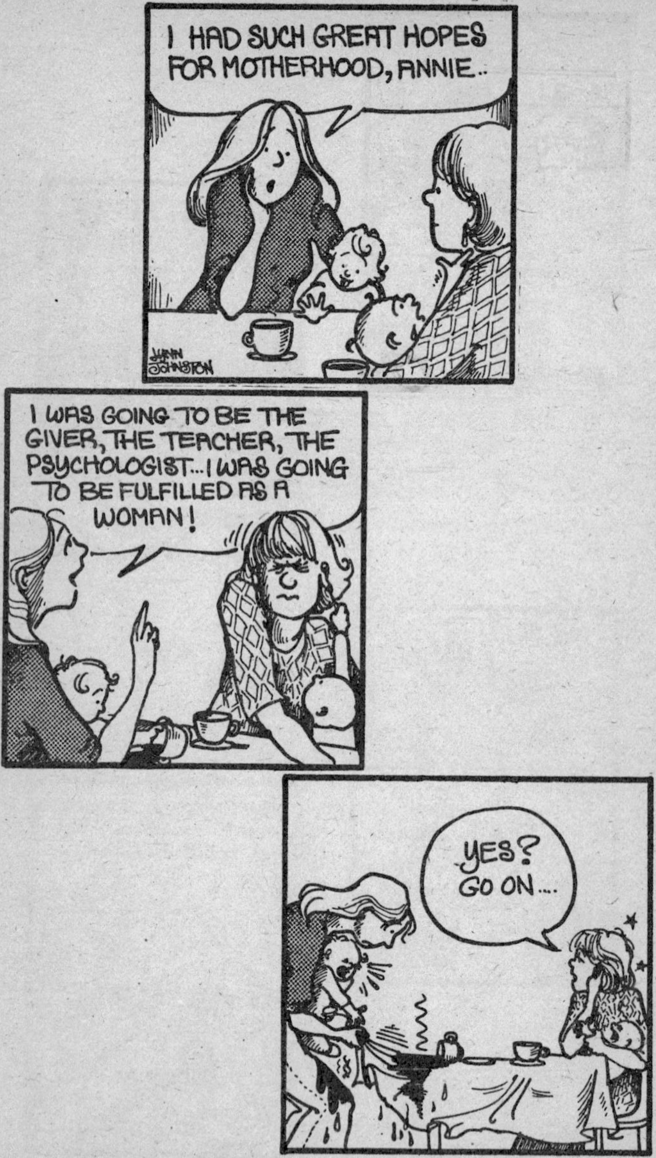
I HAD SUCH GREAT HOPES FOR MOTHERHOOD, ANNIE..
LYNN JOHNSTON
I WAS GOING TO BE THE GIVER, THE TEACHER, THE PSYCHOLOGIST...I WAS GOING TO BE FULFILLED AS A WOMAN!
YES? GO ON....

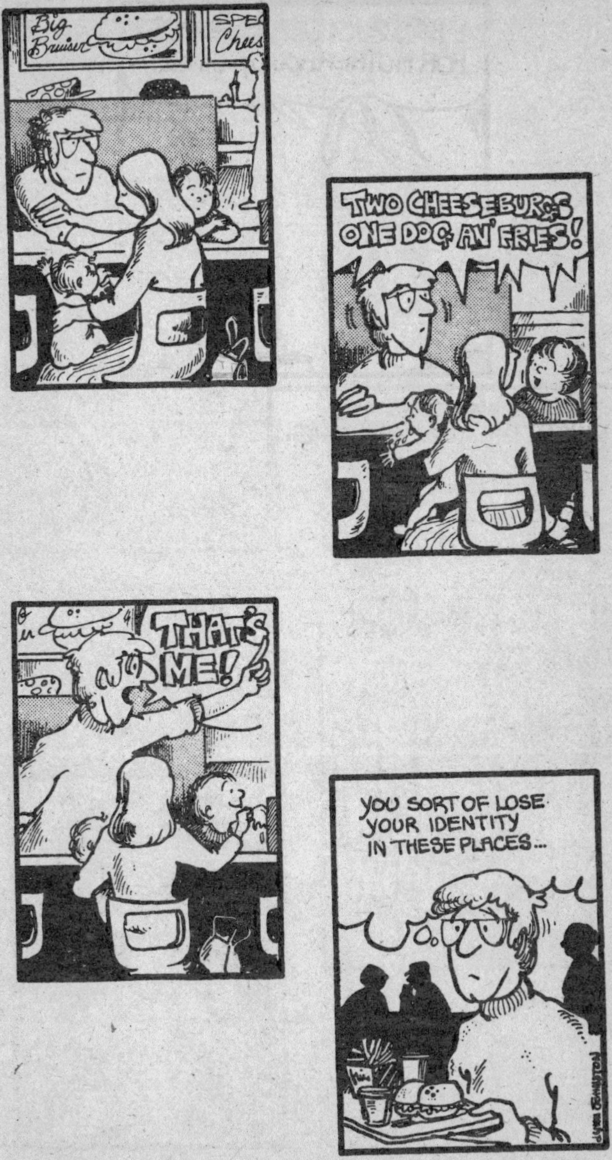
Big Bruiser
TWO CHEESEBURGS ONE DOG AN' FRIES!
THAT'S ME!
YOU SORT OF LOSE YOUR IDENTITY IN THESE PLACES...

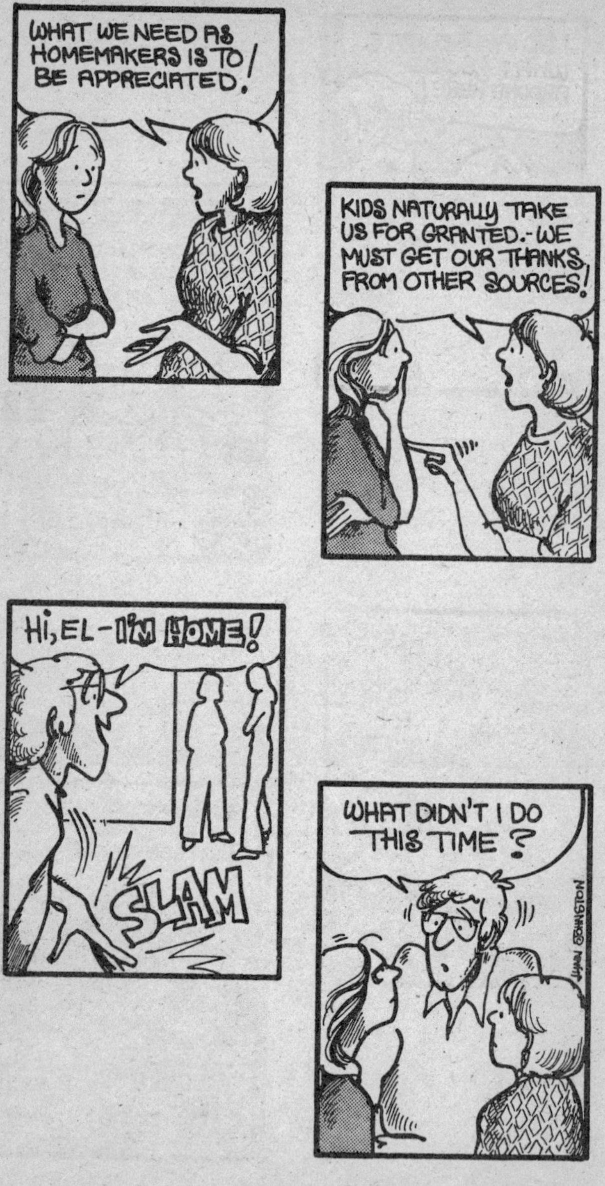
WHAT WE NEED AS HOMEMAKERS IS TO BE APPRECIATED!
KIDS NATURALLY TAKE US FOR GRANTED.-WE MUST GET OUR THANKS FROM OTHER SOURCES!
HI, EL-I'M HOME!
SLAM
WHAT DIDN'T I DO THIS TIME ?
LYNN JOHNSTON

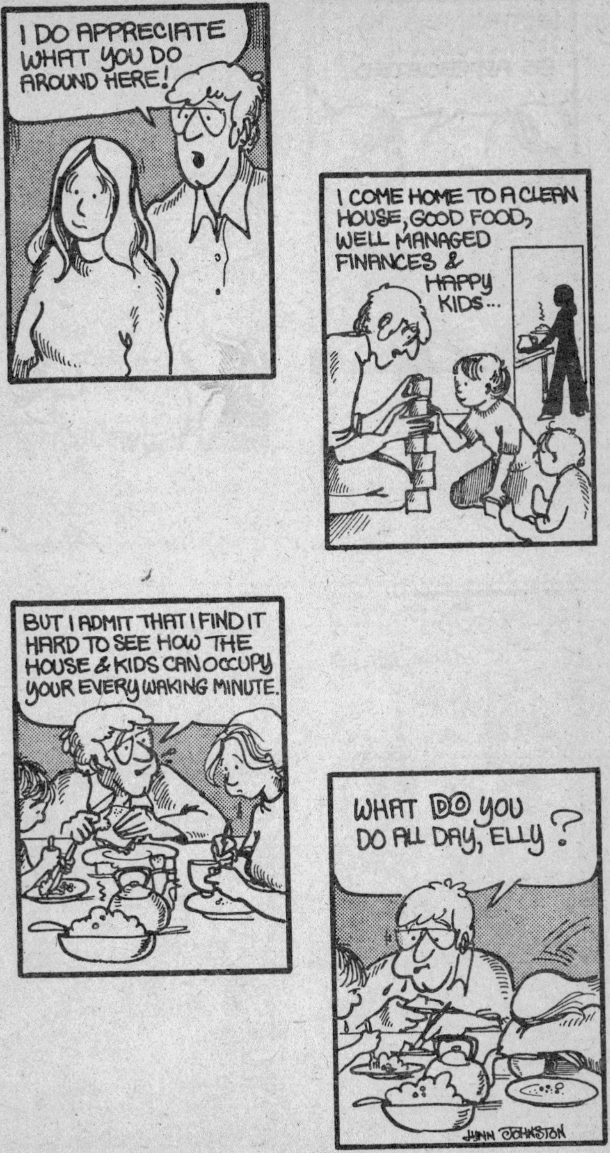
I DO APPRECIATE WHAT YOU DO AROUND HERE!
I COME HOME TO A CLEAN HOUSE, GOOD FOOD, WELL MANAGED FINANCES & HAPPY KIDS...
BUT I ADMIT THAT I FIND IT HARD TO SEE HOW THE HOUSE & KIDS CAN OCCUPY YOUR EVERY WAKING MINUTE.
WHAT DO YOU DO ALL DAY, ELLY?
LYNN JOHNSTON

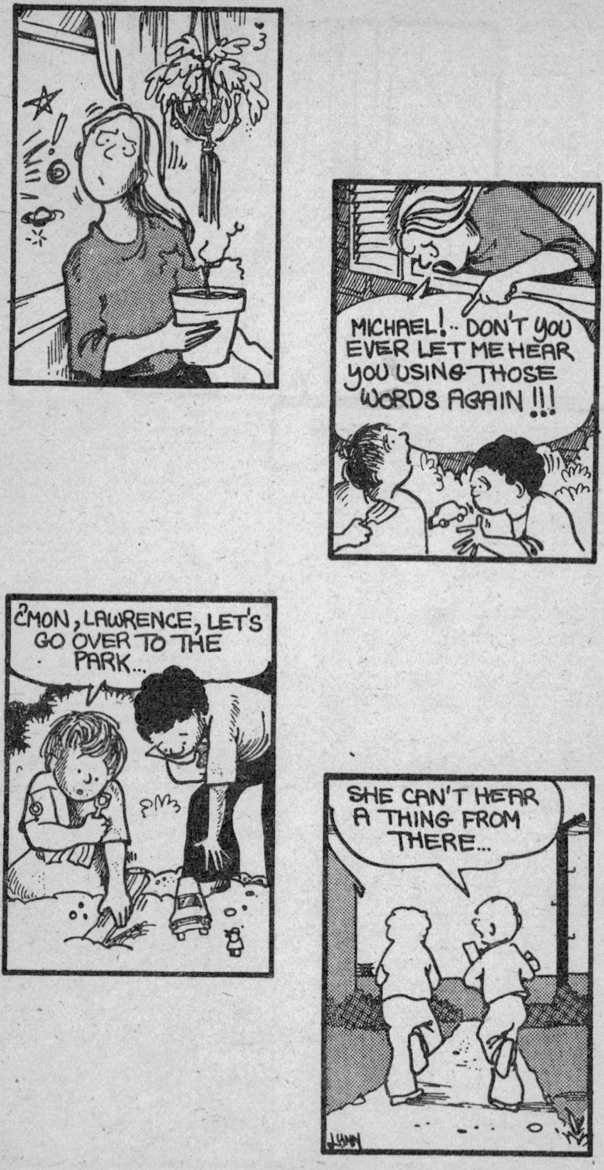
MICHAEL!.. DON'T YOU EVER LET ME HEAR YOU USING THOSE WORDS AGAIN!!!
C'MON, LAWRENCE, LET'S GO OVER TO THE PARK...
SHE CAN'T HEAR A THING FROM THERE...
LYNN

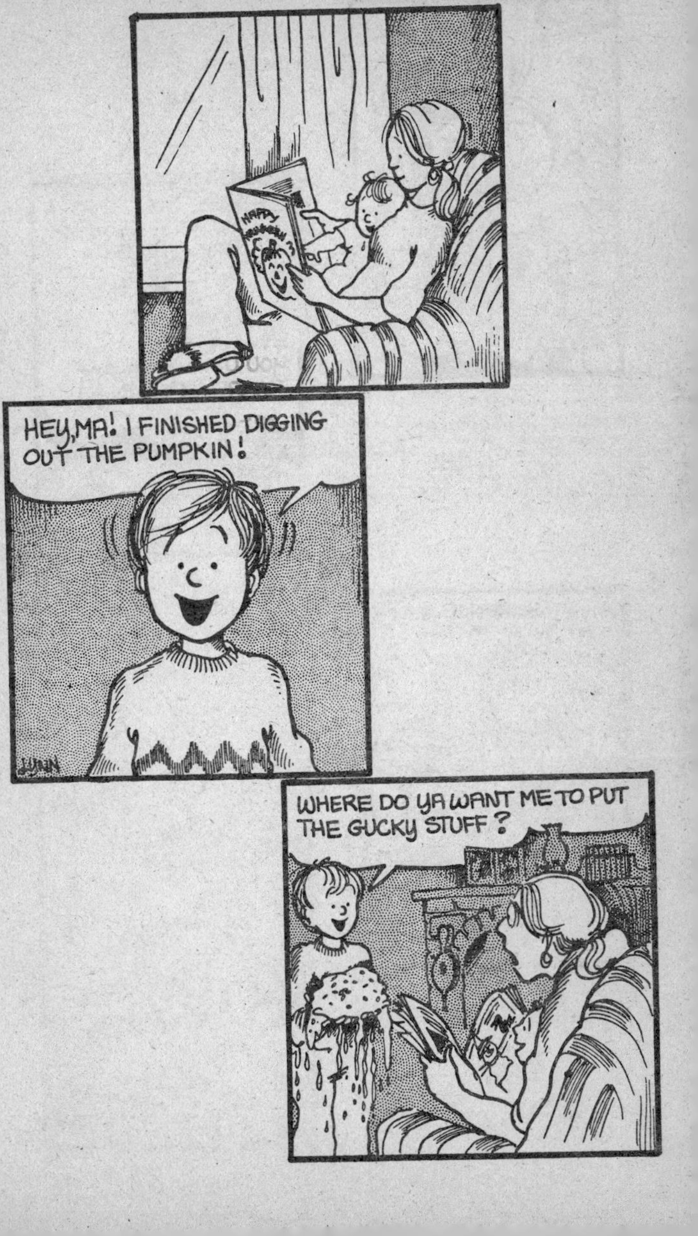
HEY, MA! I FINISHED DIGGING OUT THE PUMPKIN!
WHERE DO YA WANT ME TO PUT THE GUCKY STUFF?

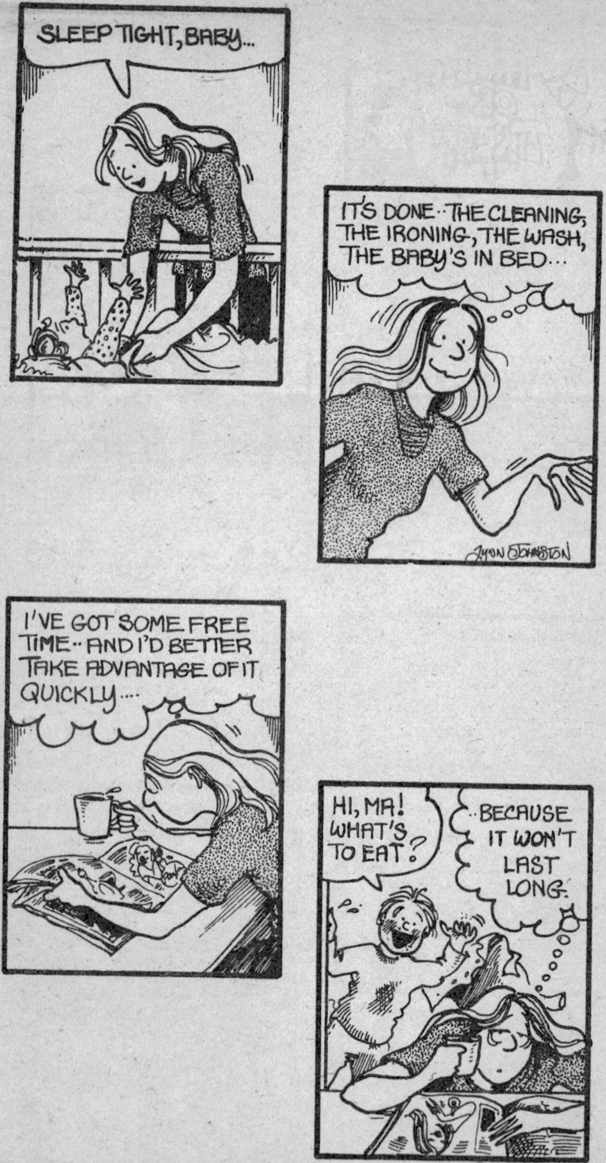
SLEEP TIGHT, BABY...
IT'S DONE·· THE CLEANING, THE IRONING, THE WASH, THE BABY'S IN BED...
LYNN JOHNSTON
I'VE GOT SOME FREE TIME·· AND I'D BETTER TAKE ADVANTAGE OF IT QUICKLY....
HI, MA! WHAT'S TO EAT?
..BECAUSE IT WON'T LAST LONG.

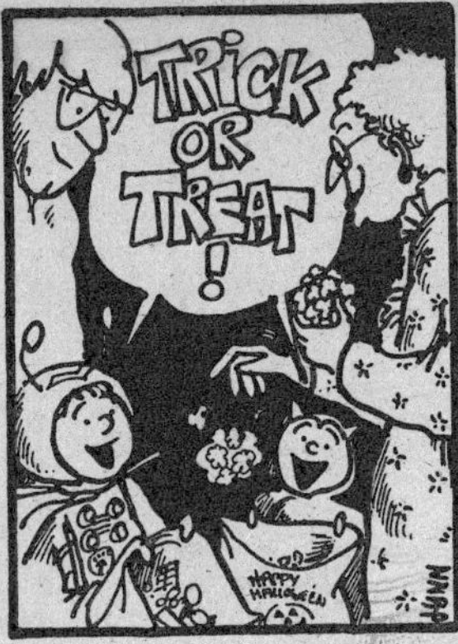
TRICK OR TREAT!

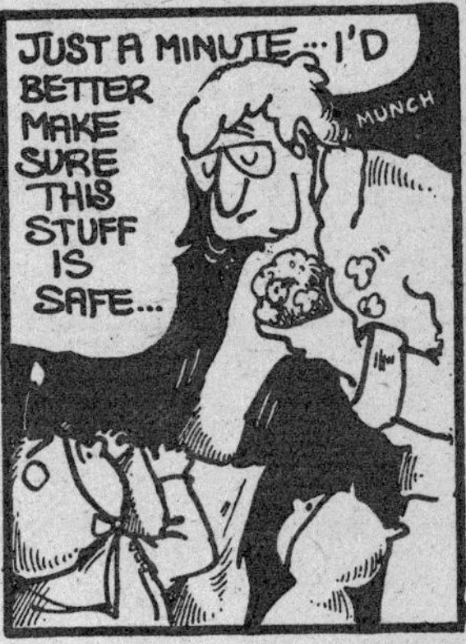
JUST A MINUTE...I'D BETTER MAKE SURE THIS STUFF IS SAFE...
MUNCH

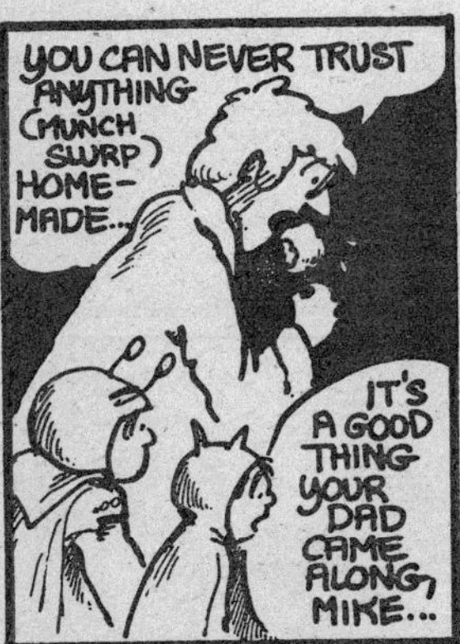
YOU CAN NEVER TRUST ANYTHING (MUNCH SLURP) HOME-MADE...
IT'S A GOOD THING YOUR DAD CAME ALONG, MIKE...

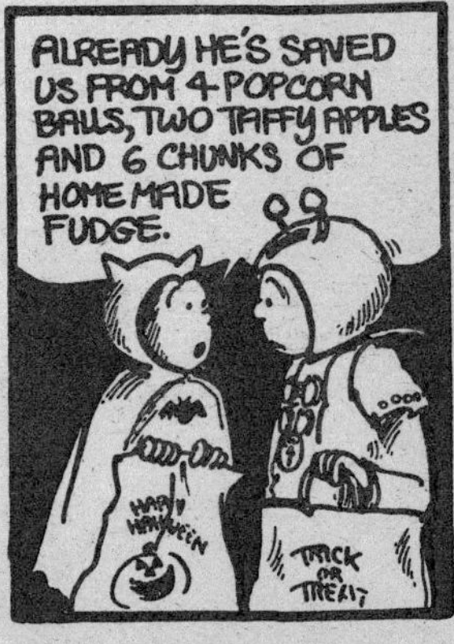
ALREADY HE'S SAVED US FROM 4 POPCORN BALLS, TWO TAFFY APPLES AND 6 CHUNKS OF HOME MADE FUDGE.

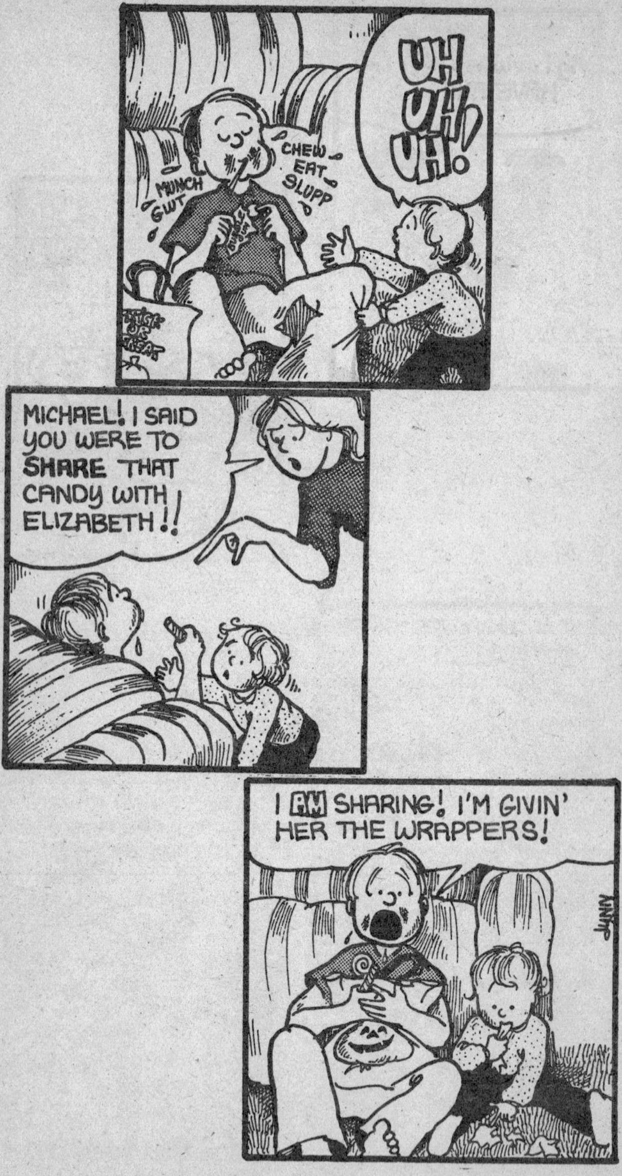

MUNCH
GWT
CHEW
EAT
SLUPP
...UH UH! UH!
TRICK OR TREAT
MICHAEL! I SAID YOU WERE TO SHARE THAT CANDY WITH ELIZABETH!!
I AM SHARING! I'M GIVIN' HER THE WRAPPERS!

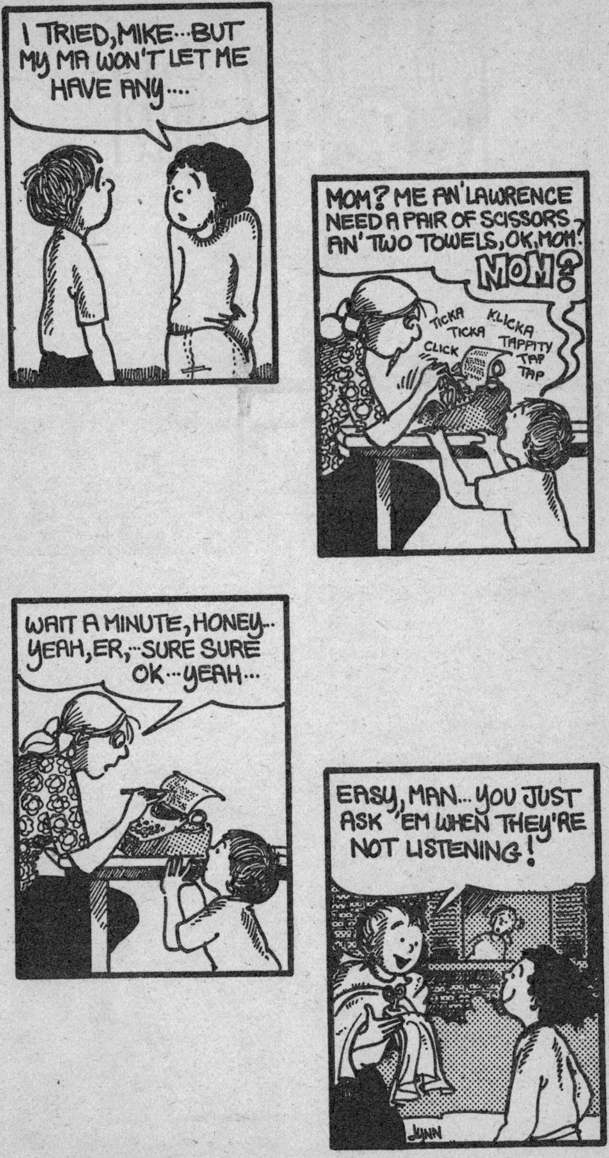
I TRIED, MIKE...BUT MY MA WON'T LET ME HAVE ANY....
MOM? ME AN' LAWRENCE NEED A PAIR OF SCISSORS AN' TWO TOWELS, OK, MOM?
MOM?
TICKA TICKA
KLICKA
CLICK
TAPPITY TAP TAP
WAIT A MINUTE, HONEY.. YEAH, ER,...SURE SURE OK...YEAH...
EASY, MAN... YOU JUST ASK 'EM WHEN THEY'RE NOT LISTENING!
LYNN

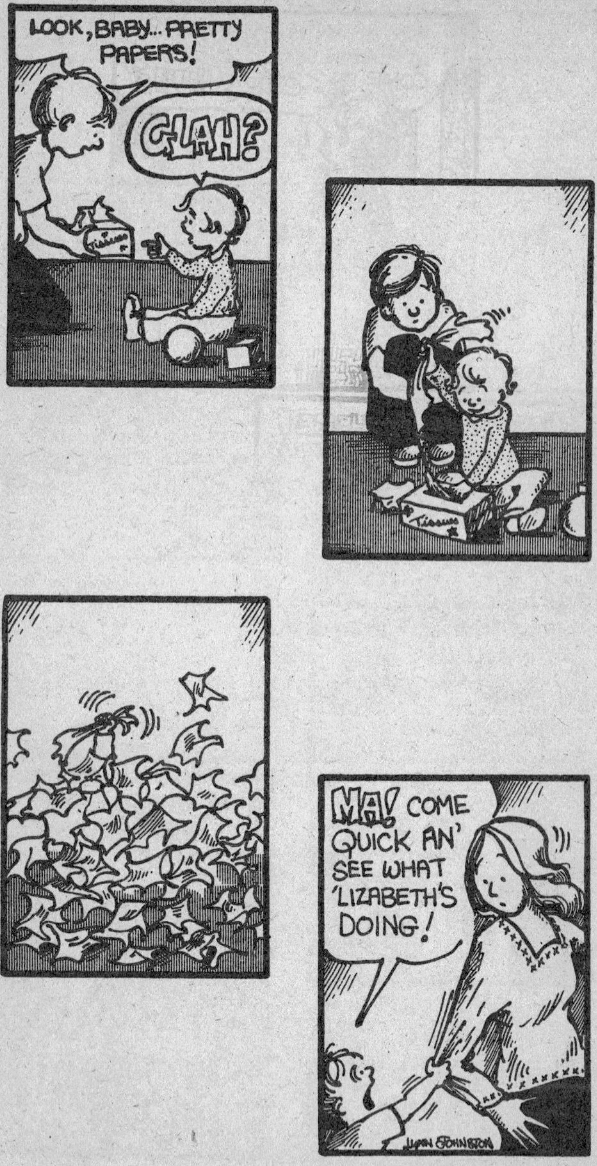
LOOK, BABY... PRETTY PAPERS!
GLAH?
Tissues
Tissues
MA! COME QUICK AN' SEE WHAT 'LIZABETH'S DOING!
LYNN JOHNSTON

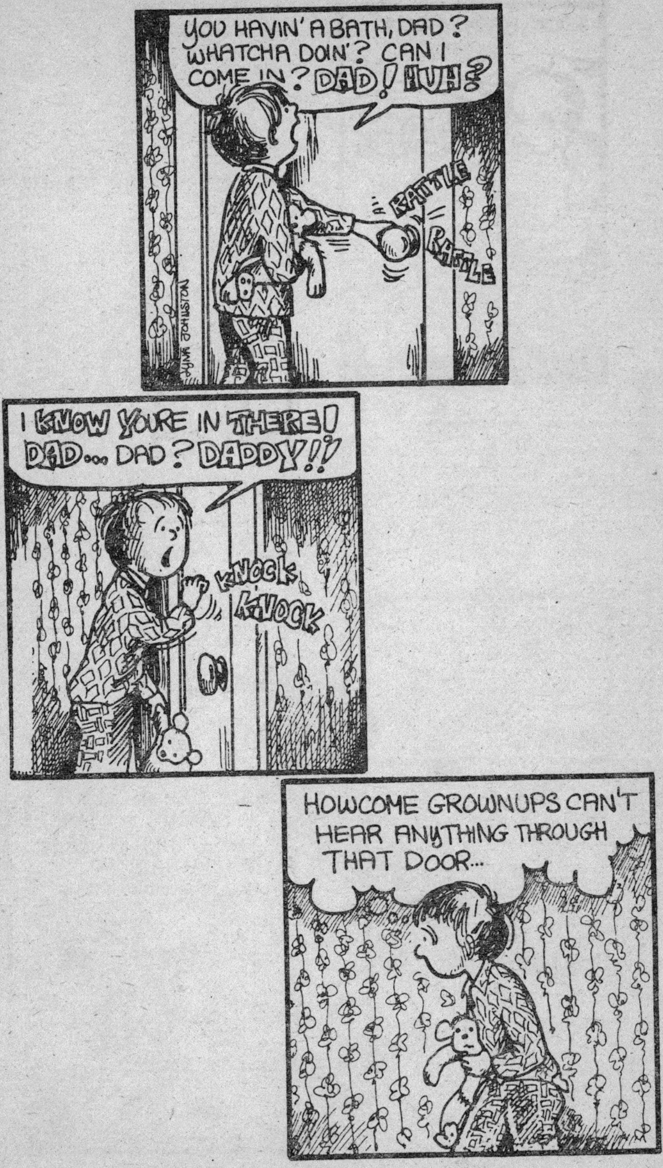
YOU HAVIN' A BATH, DAD? WHATCHA DOIN'? CAN I COME IN? DAD! HUH?
RATTLE
RATTLE
LYNN JOHNSTON
I KNOW YOURE IN THERE! DAD... DAD? DADDY!!
KNOCK
KNOCK
HOWCOME GROWNUPS CAN'T HEAR ANYTHING THROUGH THAT DOOR...

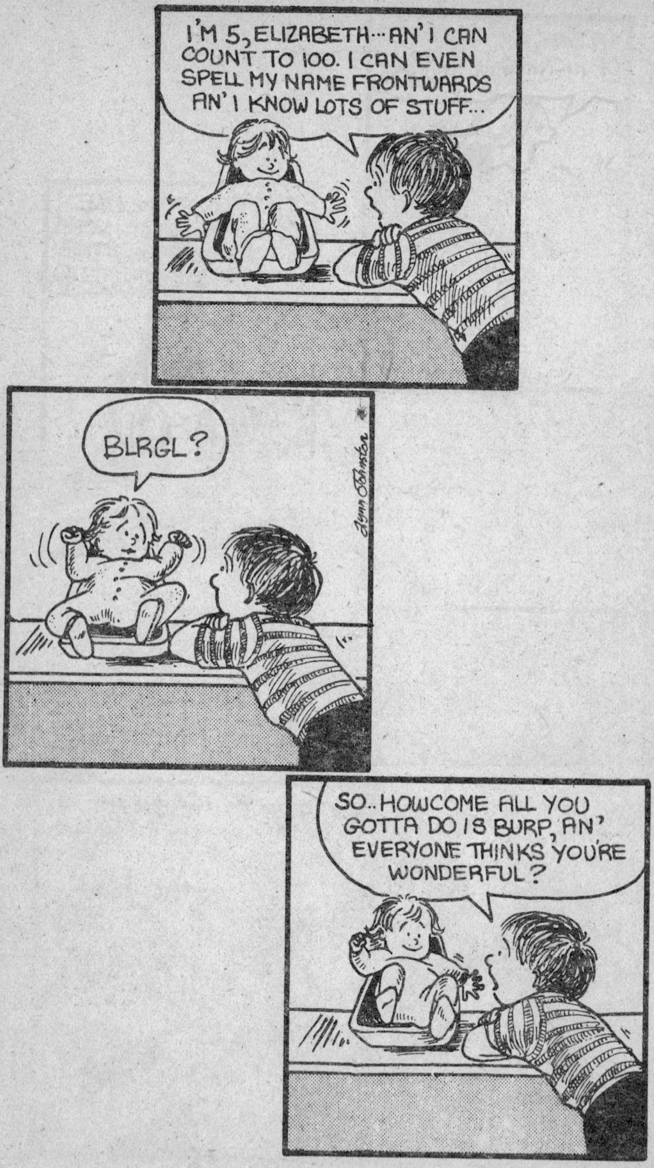
I'M 5, ELIZABETH··· AN' I CAN COUNT TO 100. I CAN EVEN SPELL MY NAME FRONTWARDS AN' I KNOW LOTS OF STUFF...
BLRGL?
Lynn Johnston
SO.. HOWCOME ALL YOU GOTTA DO IS BURP, AN' EVERYONE THINKS YOU'RE WONDERFUL?

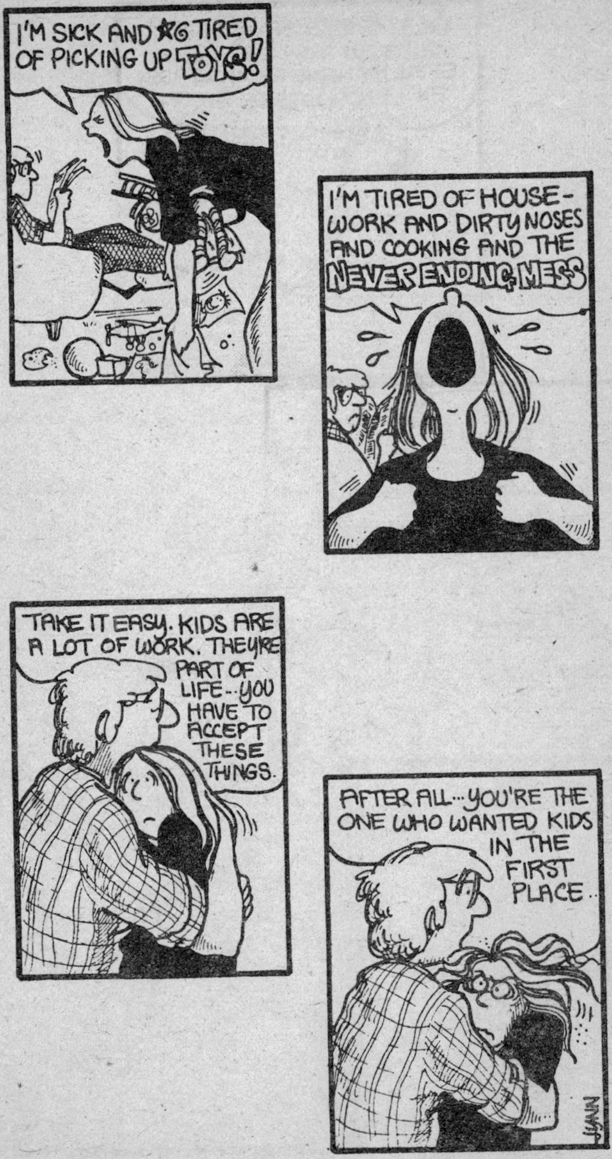
I'M SICK AND ★6 TIRED OF PICKING UP TOYS!
I'M TIRED OF HOUSE-WORK AND DIRTY NOSES AND COOKING AND THE NEVER ENDING MESS
TAKE IT EASY. KIDS ARE A LOT OF WORK. THEY'RE PART OF LIFE--YOU HAVE TO ACCEPT THESE THINGS.
AFTER ALL...YOU'RE THE ONE WHO WANTED KIDS IN THE FIRST PLACE..
LYNN

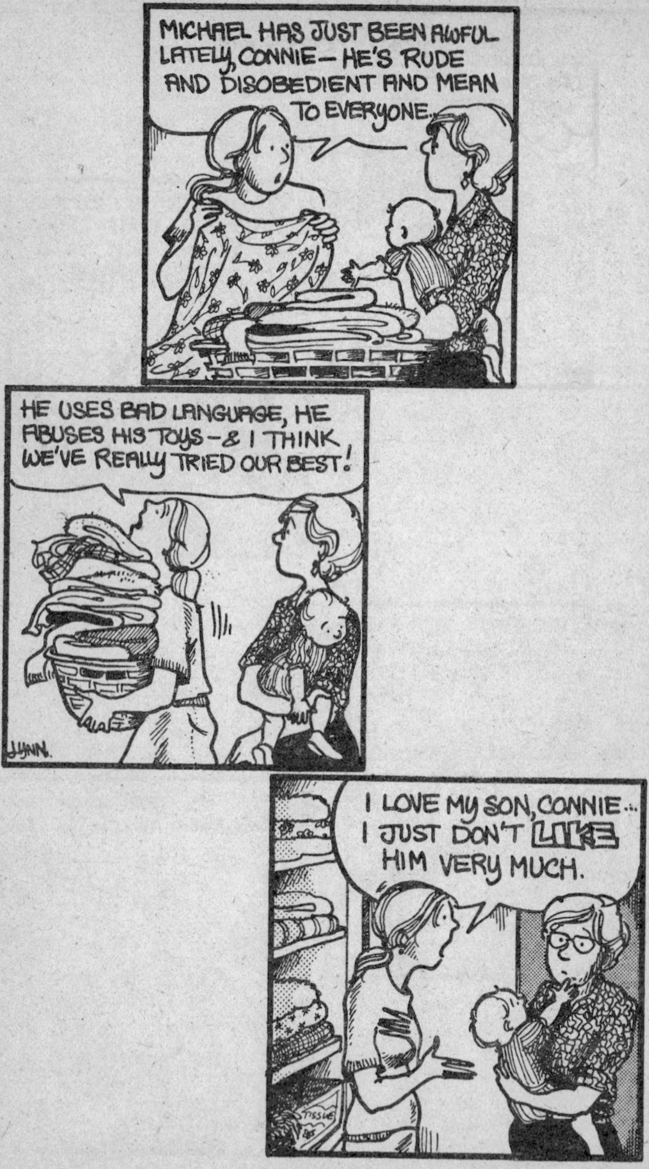
MICHAEL HAS JUST BEEN AWFUL LATELY, CONNIE— HE'S RUDE AND DISOBEDIENT AND MEAN TO EVERYONE.
HE USES BAD LANGUAGE, HE ABUSES HIS TOYS—& I THINK WE'VE REALLY TRIED OUR BEST!
LYNN.
I LOVE MY SON, CONNIE... I JUST DON'T LIKE HIM VERY MUCH.
TISSUE

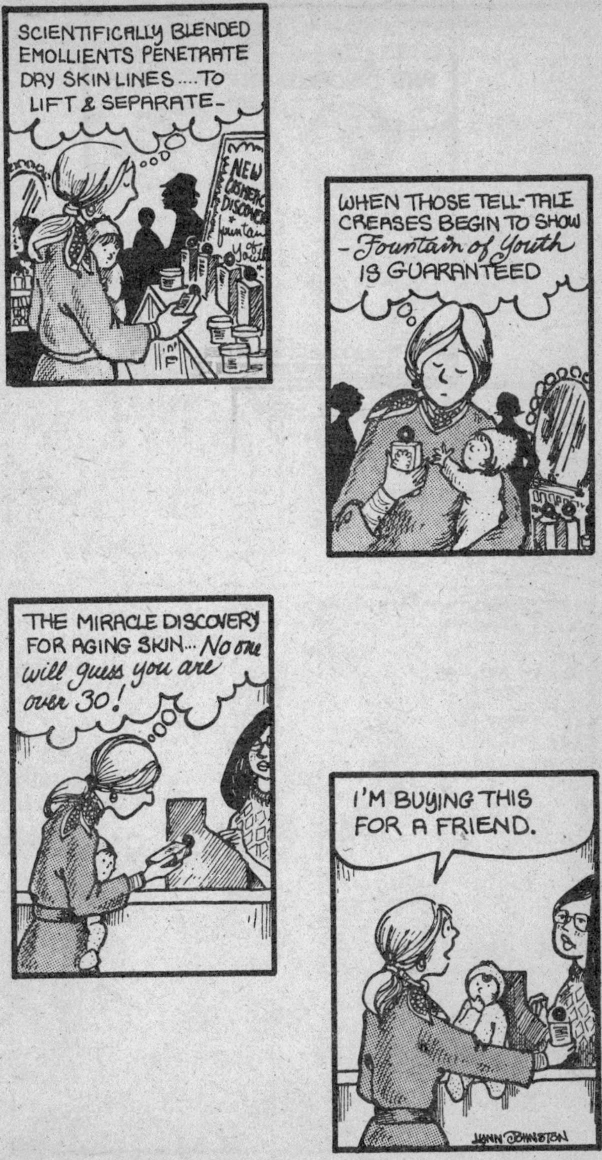
SCIENTIFICALLY BLENDED EMOLLIENTS PENETRATE DRY SKIN LINES.... TO LIFT & SEPARATE-
WHEN THOSE TELL-TALE CREASES BEGIN TO SHOW - Fountain of Youth IS GUARANTEED
THE MIRACLE DISCOVERY FOR AGING SKIN... No one will guess you are over 30!
I'M BUYING THIS FOR A FRIEND.
LYNN JOHNSTON

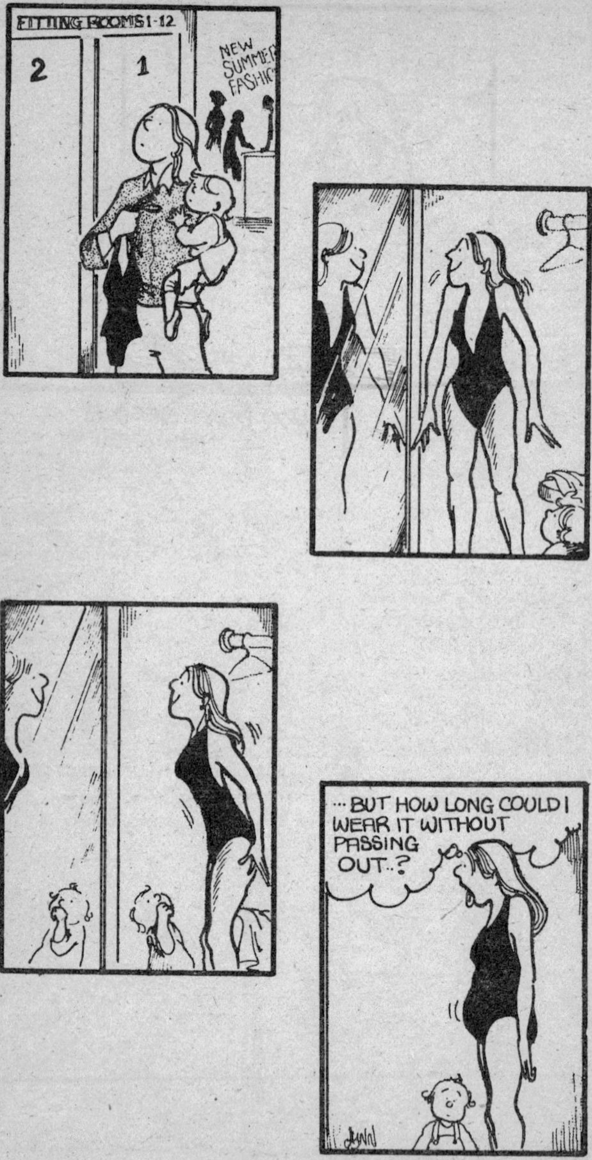
FITTING ROOMS 1-12
2
1
NEW
...BUT HOW LONG COULD I WEAR IT WITHOUT PASSING OUT..?

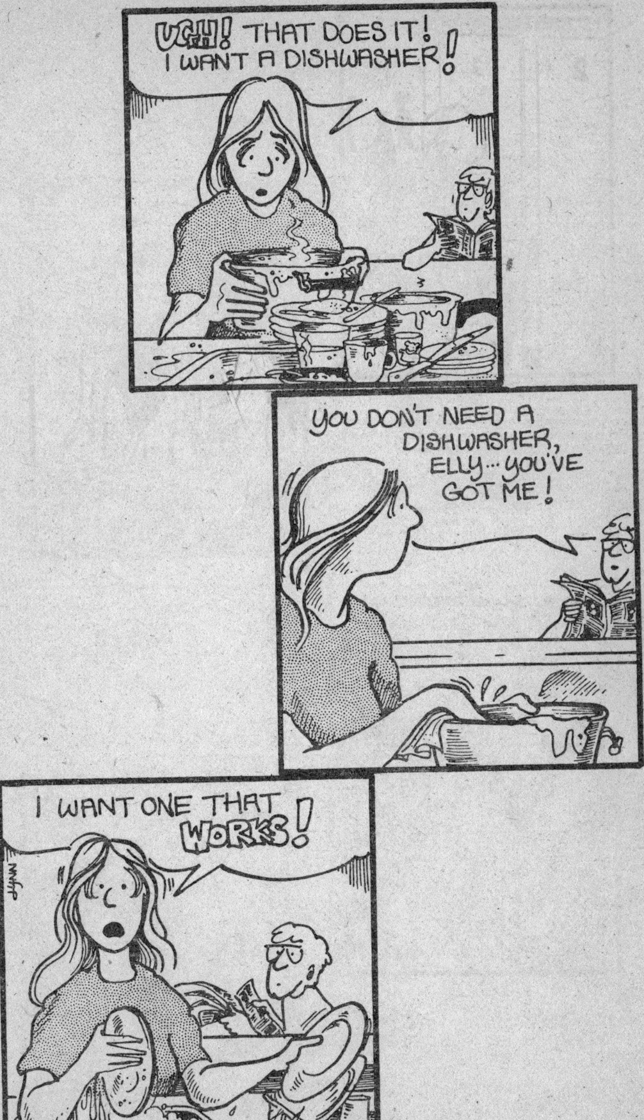
UGH! THAT DOES IT! I WANT A DISHWASHER!
YOU DON'T NEED A DISHWASHER, ELLY... YOU'VE GOT ME!
I WANT ONE THAT WORKS!

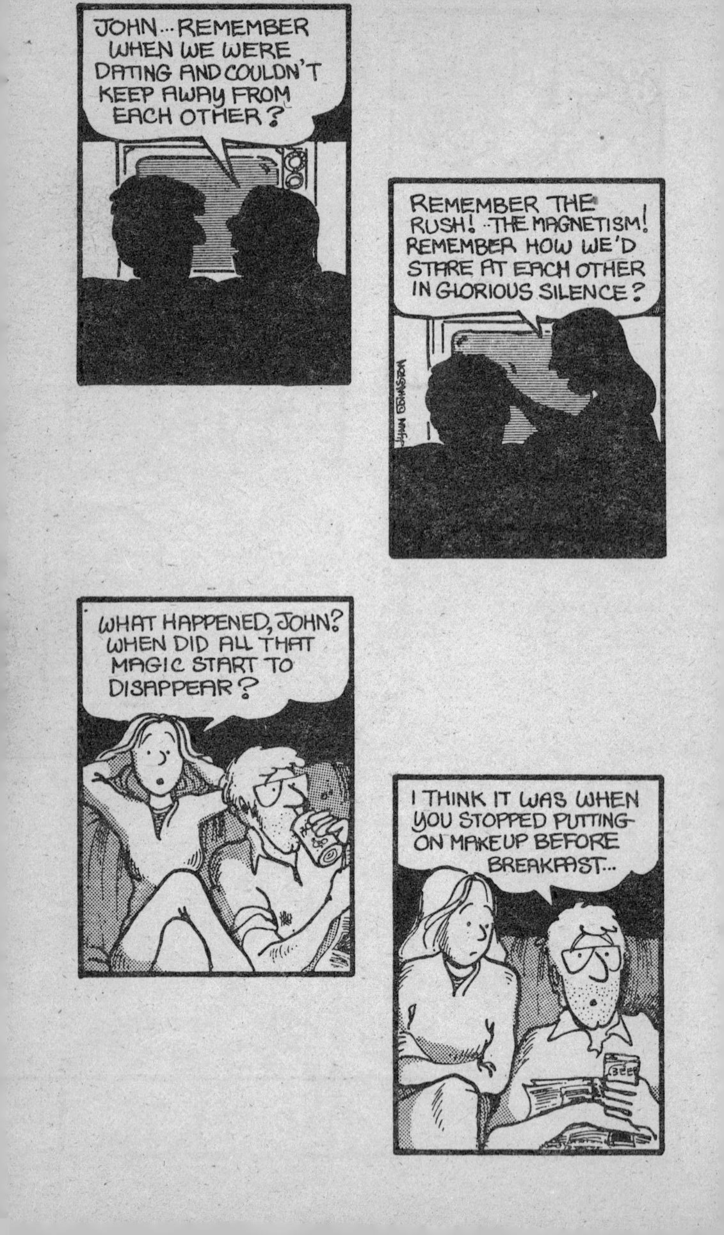
JOHN...REMEMBER WHEN WE WERE DATING AND COULDN'T KEEP AWAY FROM EACH OTHER?
REMEMBER THE RUSH! -THE MAGNETISM! REMEMBER HOW WE'D STARE AT EACH OTHER IN GLORIOUS SILENCE?
WHAT HAPPENED, JOHN? WHEN DID ALL THAT MAGIC START TO DISAPPEAR?
I THINK IT WAS WHEN YOU STOPPED PUTTING ON MAKEUP BEFORE BREAKFAST...
BEER

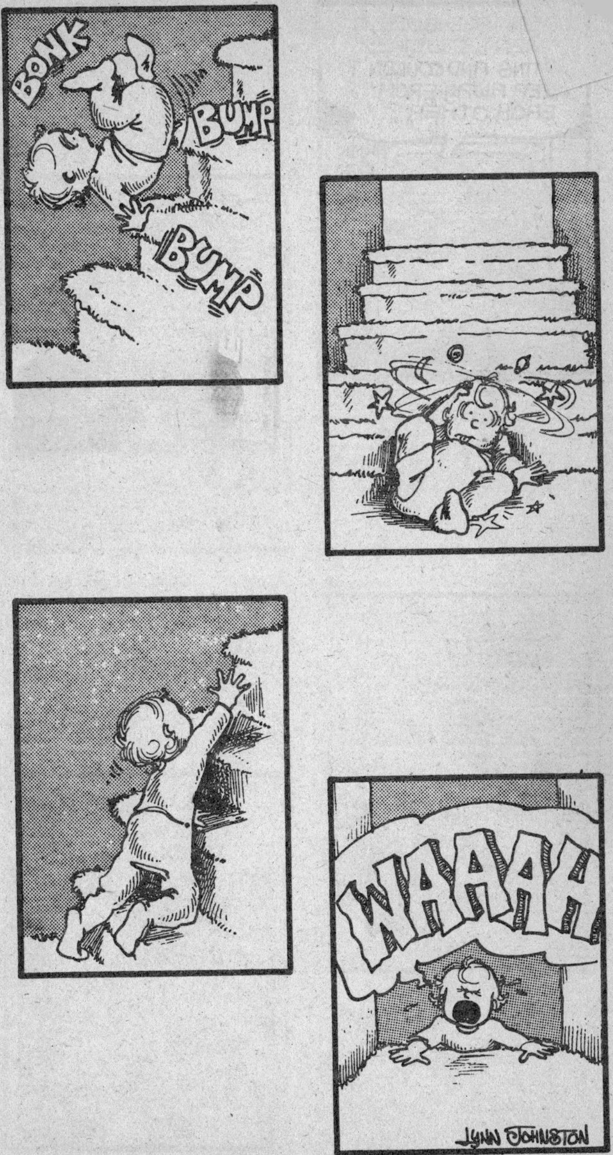
BONK
BUMP
BUMP
WAAAH
LYNN JOHNSTON

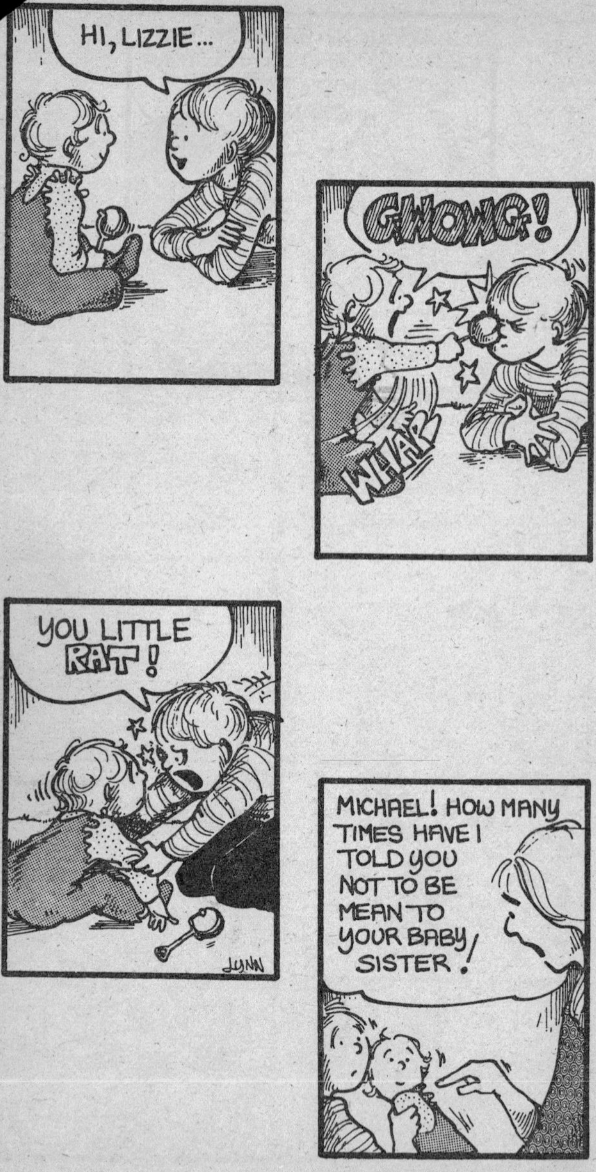
HI, LIZZIE...
GWONG!
WHAP
YOU LITTLE RAT!
MICHAEL! HOW MANY TIMES HAVE I TOLD YOU NOT TO BE MEAN TO YOUR BABY SISTER!
LYNN

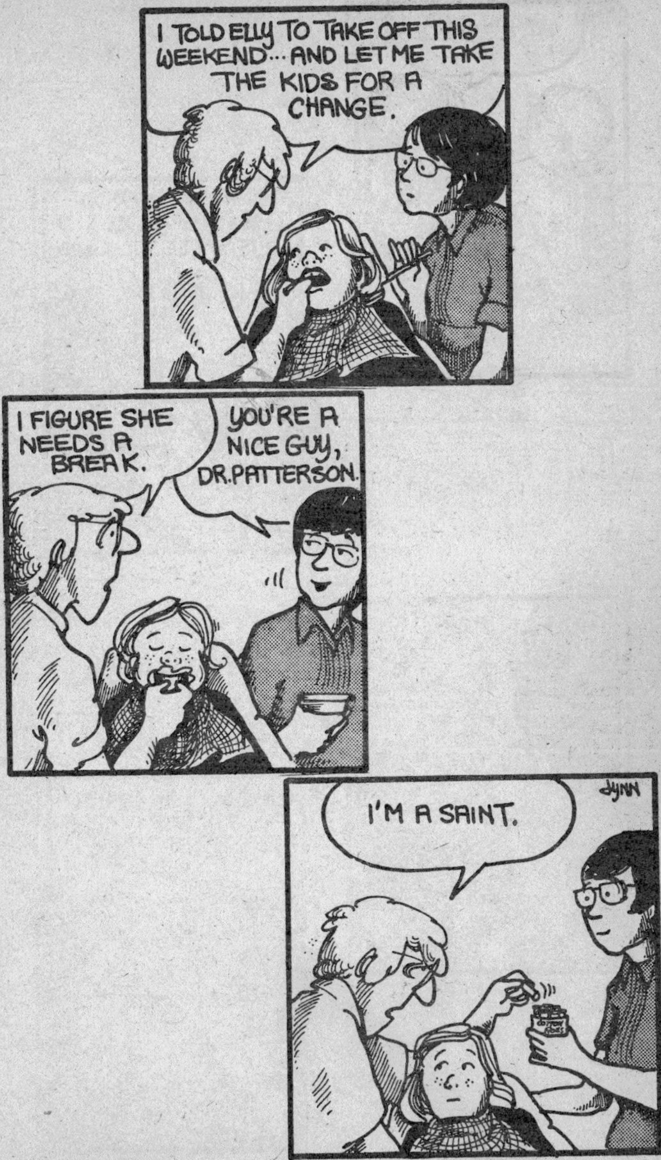
I TOLD ELLY TO TAKE OFF THIS WEEKEND... AND LET ME TAKE THE KIDS FOR A CHANGE.
I FIGURE SHE NEEDS A BREAK.
YOU'RE A NICE GUY, DR. PATTERSON.
I'M A SAINT.
Lynn

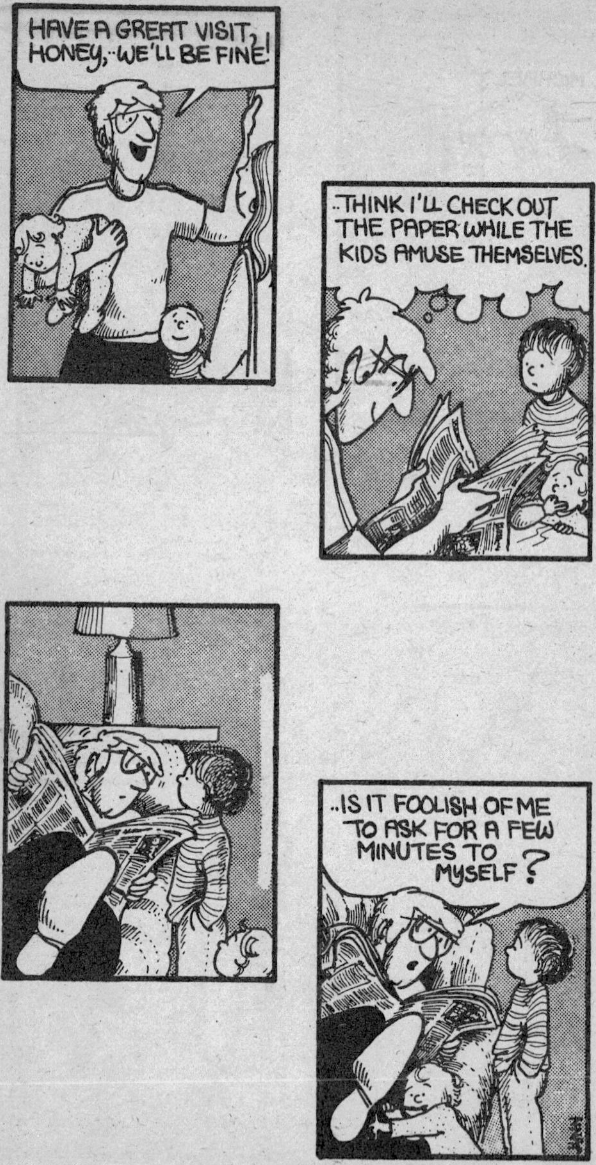
HAVE A GREAT VISIT, HONEY,--WE'LL BE FINE!
..THINK I'LL CHECK OUT THE PAPER WHILE THE KIDS AMUSE THEMSELVES.
..IS IT FOOLISH OF ME TO ASK FOR A FEW MINUTES TO MYSELF?

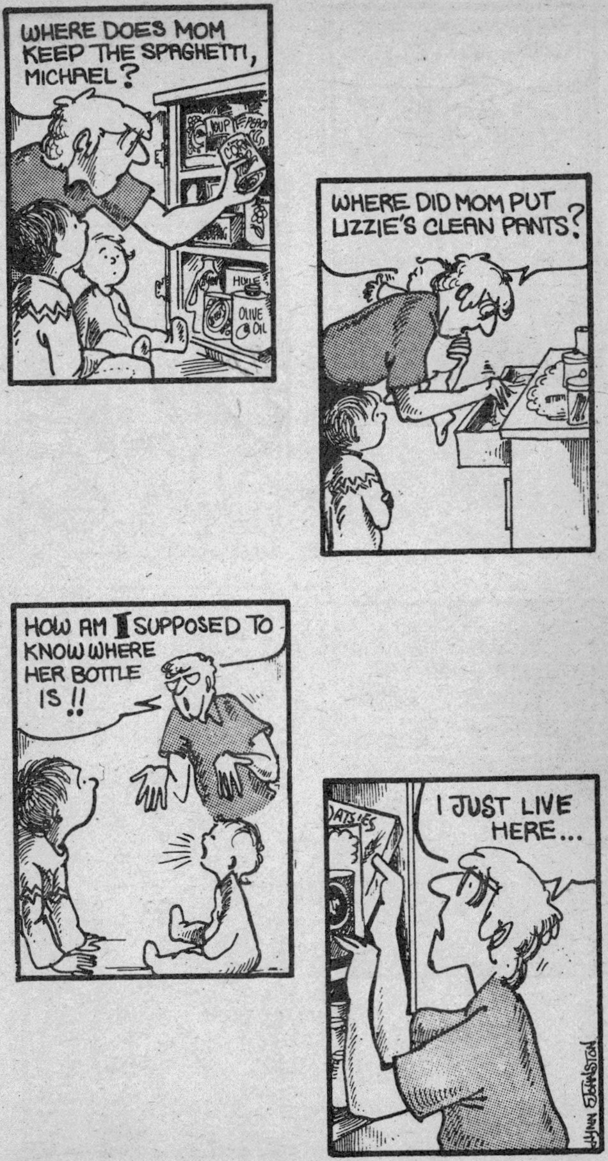
WHERE DOES MOM KEEP THE SPAGHETTI, MICHAEL?
WHERE DID MOM PUT LIZZIE'S CLEAN PANTS?
HOW AM I SUPPOSED TO KNOW WHERE HER BOTTLE IS!!
I JUST LIVE HERE...

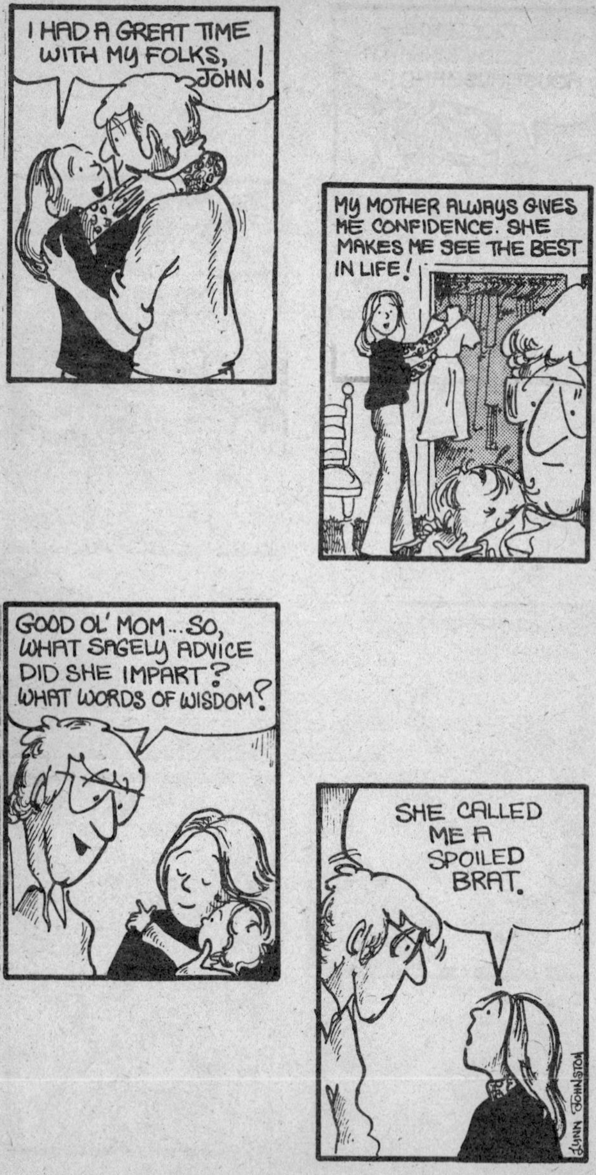
I HAD A GREAT TIME WITH MY FOLKS, JOHN!
MY MOTHER ALWAYS GIVES ME CONFIDENCE. SHE MAKES ME SEE THE BEST IN LIFE!
GOOD OL' MOM...SO, WHAT SAGELY ADVICE DID SHE IMPART? WHAT WORDS OF WISDOM?
SHE CALLED ME A SPOILED BRAT.
LYNN JOHNSTON

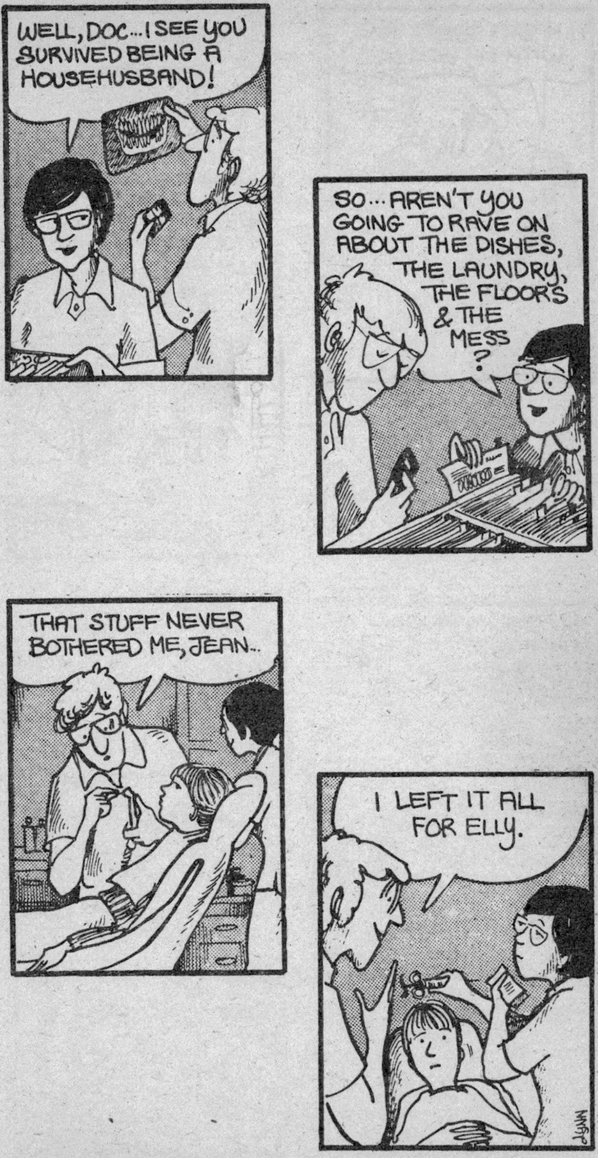
WELL, DOC...I SEE YOU SURVIVED BEING A HOUSEHUSBAND!
SO... AREN'T YOU GOING TO RAVE ON ABOUT THE DISHES, THE LAUNDRY, THE FLOORS & THE MESS?
THAT STUFF NEVER BOTHERED ME, JEAN..
I LEFT IT ALL FOR ELLY.
LYNN

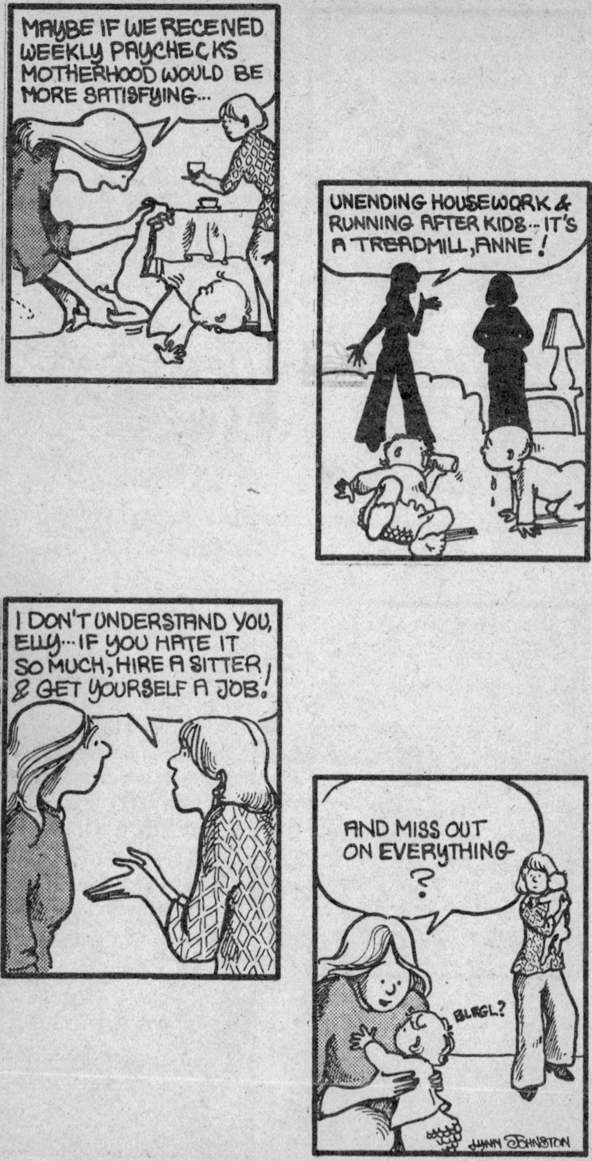
MAYBE IF WE RECENED WEEKLY PAYCHECKS MOTHERHOOD WOULD BE MORE SATISFYING...
UNENDING HOUSEWORK & RUNNING AFTER KIDS... IT'S A TREADMILL, ANNE!
I DON'T UNDERSTAND YOU, ELLY... IF YOU HATE IT SO MUCH, HIRE A SITTER, & GET YOURSELF A JOB!
AND MISS OUT ON EVERYTHING ?
BLRGL?
LYNN JOHNSTON

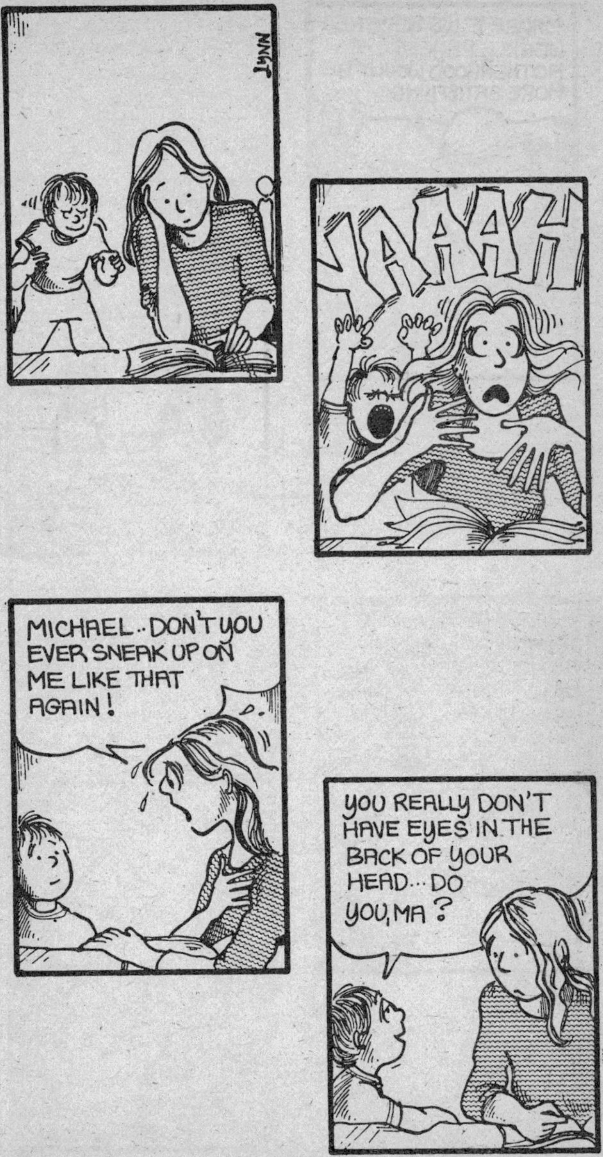
LYNN
YAAAH
MICHAEL.. DON'T YOU EVER SNEAK UP ON ME LIKE THAT AGAIN!
YOU REALLY DON'T HAVE EYES IN THE BACK OF YOUR HEAD... DO YOU, MA?

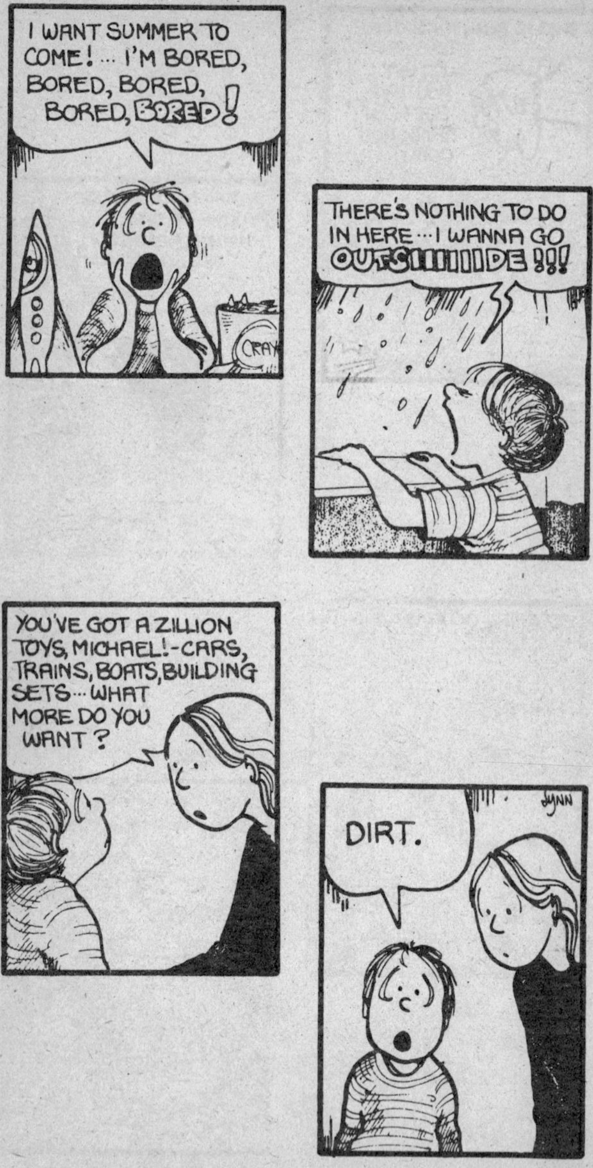
I WANT SUMMER TO COME! ... I'M BORED, BORED, BORED, BORED, BORED!
THERE'S NOTHING TO DO IN HERE ... I WANNA GO OUTSIIIIIIIDE!!!
YOU'VE GOT A ZILLION TOYS, MICHAEL! - CARS, TRAINS, BOATS, BUILDING SETS ... WHAT MORE DO YOU WANT?
DIRT.
LYNN

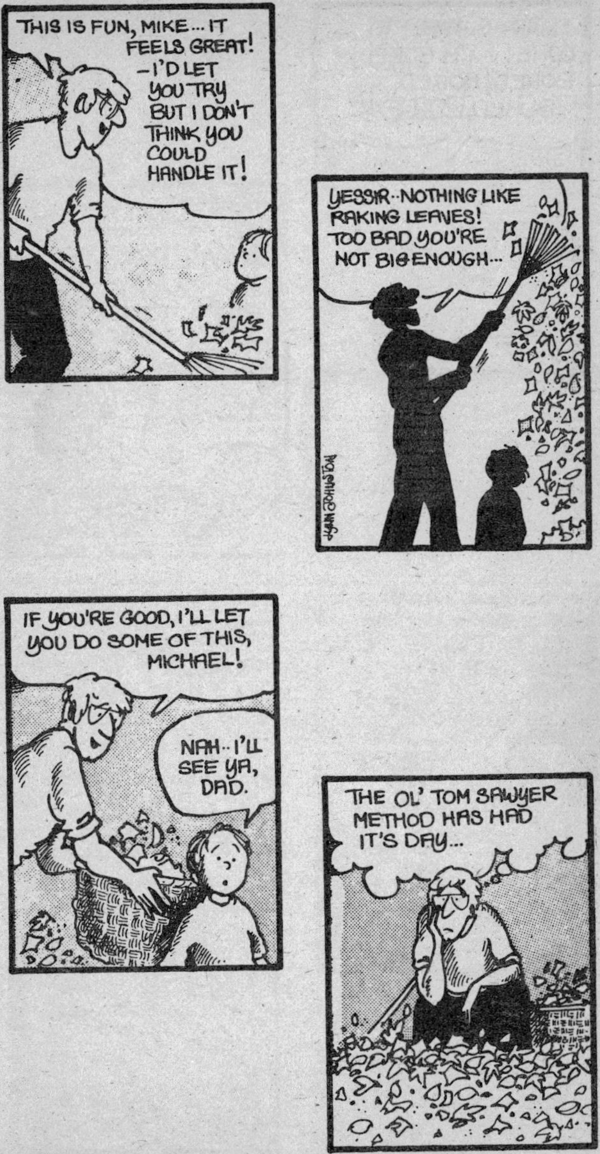
THIS IS FUN, MIKE... IT FEELS GREAT! –I'D LET YOU TRY BUT I DON'T THINK YOU COULD HANDLE IT!
YESSIR.. NOTHING LIKE RAKING LEAVES! TOO BAD YOU'RE NOT BIG ENOUGH...
LYNN JOHNSTON
IF YOU'RE GOOD, I'LL LET YOU DO SOME OF THIS, MICHAEL!
NAH.. I'LL SEE YA, DAD.
THE OL' TOM SAWYER METHOD HAS HAD IT'S DAY...

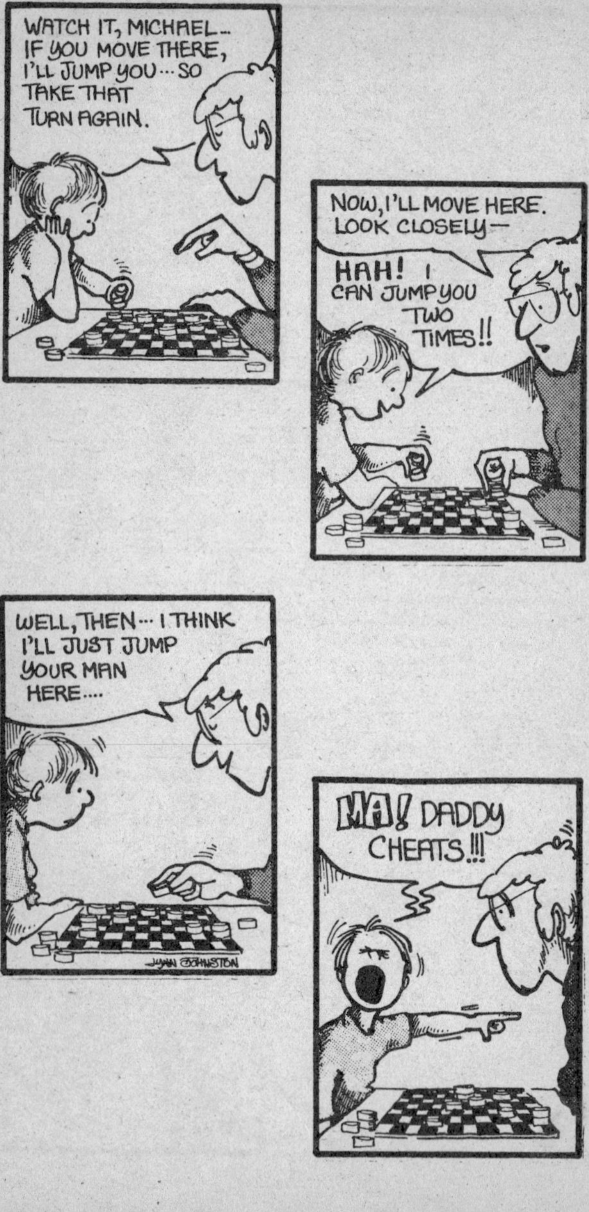
WATCH IT, MICHAEL... IF YOU MOVE THERE, I'LL JUMP YOU... SO TAKE THAT TURN AGAIN.
NOW, I'LL MOVE HERE. LOOK CLOSELY—
HAH! I CAN JUMP YOU TWO TIMES!!
WELL, THEN... I THINK I'LL JUST JUMP YOUR MAN HERE....
LYNN JOHNSTON
MA! DADDY CHEATS!!!

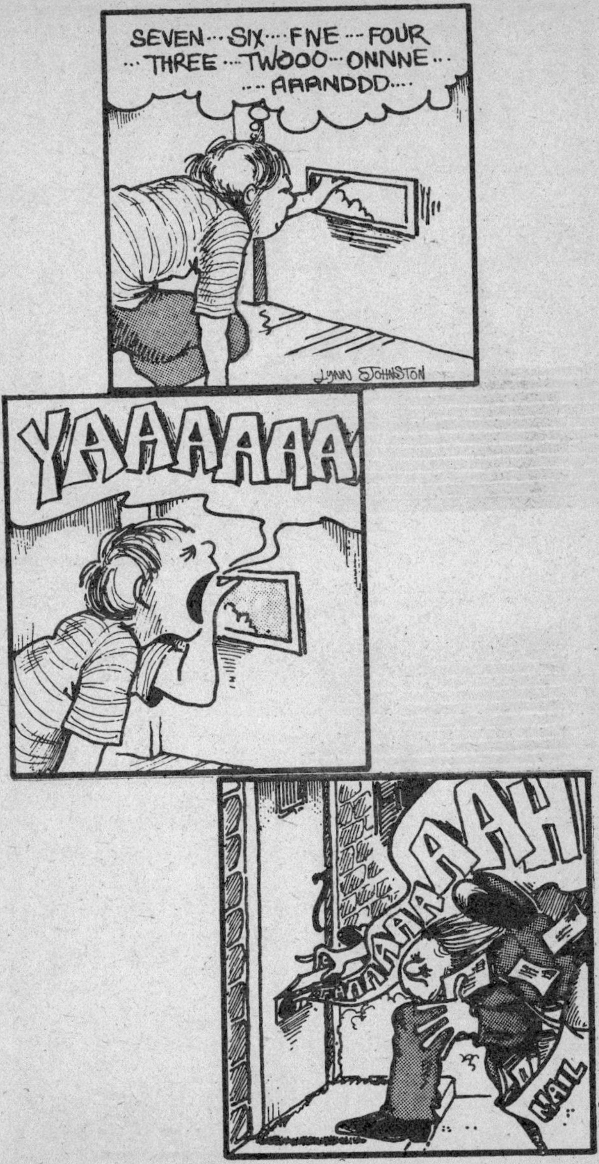

SEVEN... SIX... FIVE ... FOUR ... THREE ... TWOOO... ONNNE... ... ARRNDDD....
LYNN JOHNSTON
YAAAAAA
AAH
MAIL

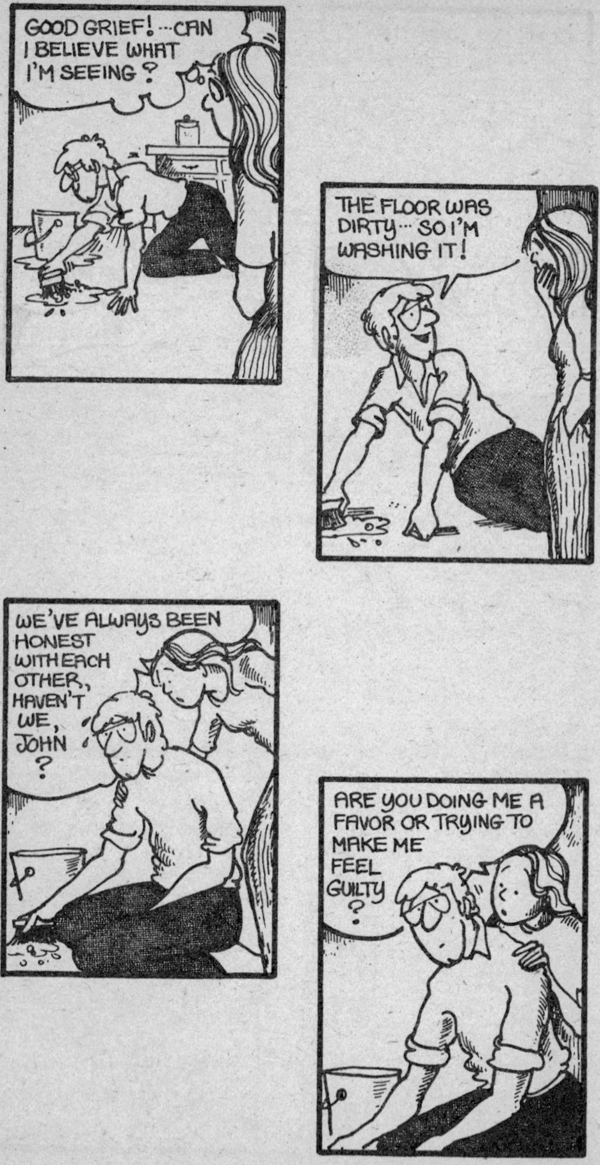
GOOD GRIEF! ...CAN I BELIEVE WHAT I'M SEEING?
THE FLOOR WAS DIRTY... SO I'M WASHING IT!
WE'VE ALWAYS BEEN HONEST WITH EACH OTHER, HAVEN'T WE, JOHN?
ARE YOU DOING ME A FAVOR OR TRYING TO MAKE ME FEEL GUILTY?

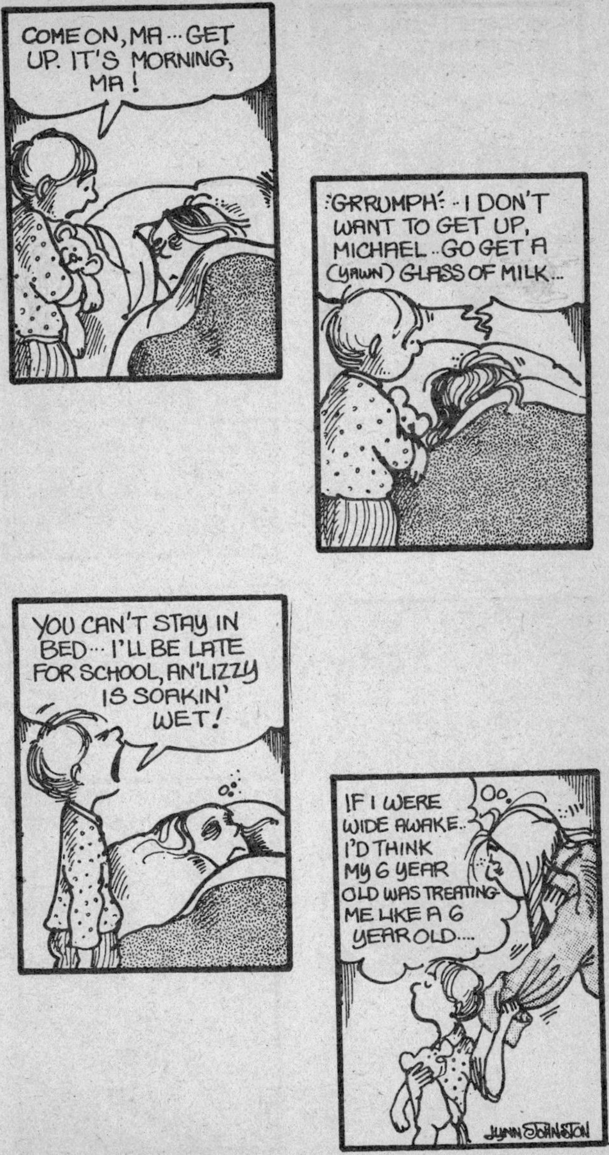
COME ON, MA ··· GET UP. IT'S MORNING, MA!
GRRUMPH ·· I DON'T WANT TO GET UP, MICHAEL .. GO GET A (YAWN) GLASS OF MILK...
YOU CAN'T STAY IN BED ··· I'LL BE LATE FOR SCHOOL, AN' LIZZY IS SOAKIN' WET!
IF I WERE WIDE AWAKE.. I'D THINK MY 6 YEAR OLD WAS TREATING ME LIKE A 6 YEAR OLD....
LYNN JOHNSTON

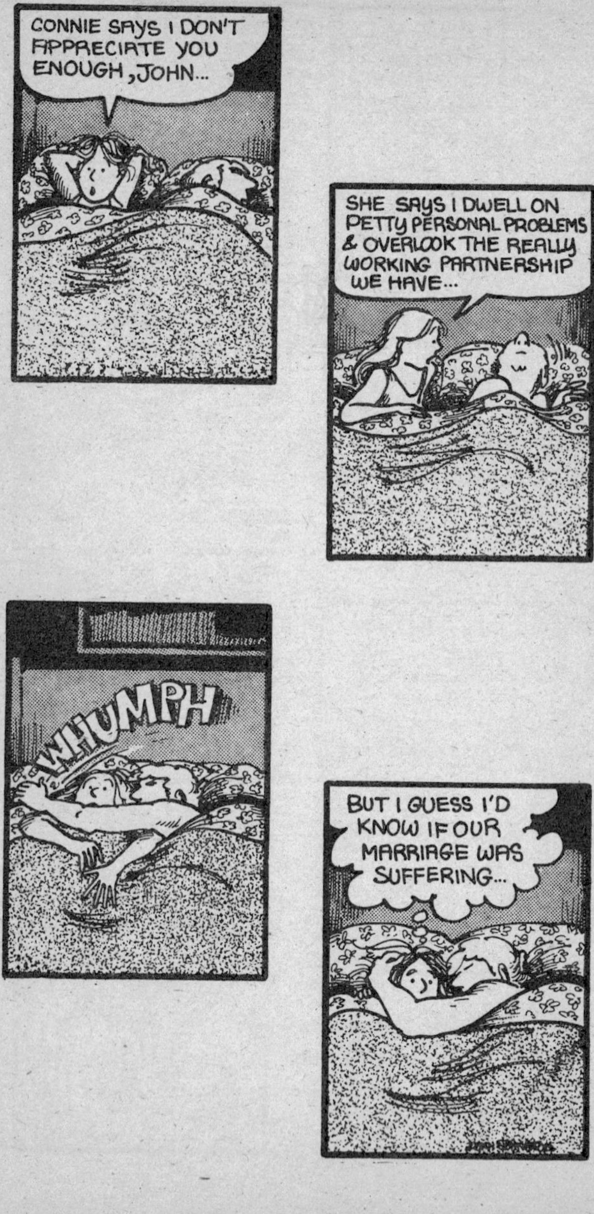
CONNIE SAYS I DON'T APPRECIATE YOU ENOUGH, JOHN...
SHE SAYS I DWELL ON PETTY PERSONAL PROBLEMS & OVERLOOK THE REALLY WORKING PARTNERSHIP WE HAVE...
WHUMPH
BUT I GUESS I'D KNOW IF OUR MARRIAGE WAS SUFFERING...

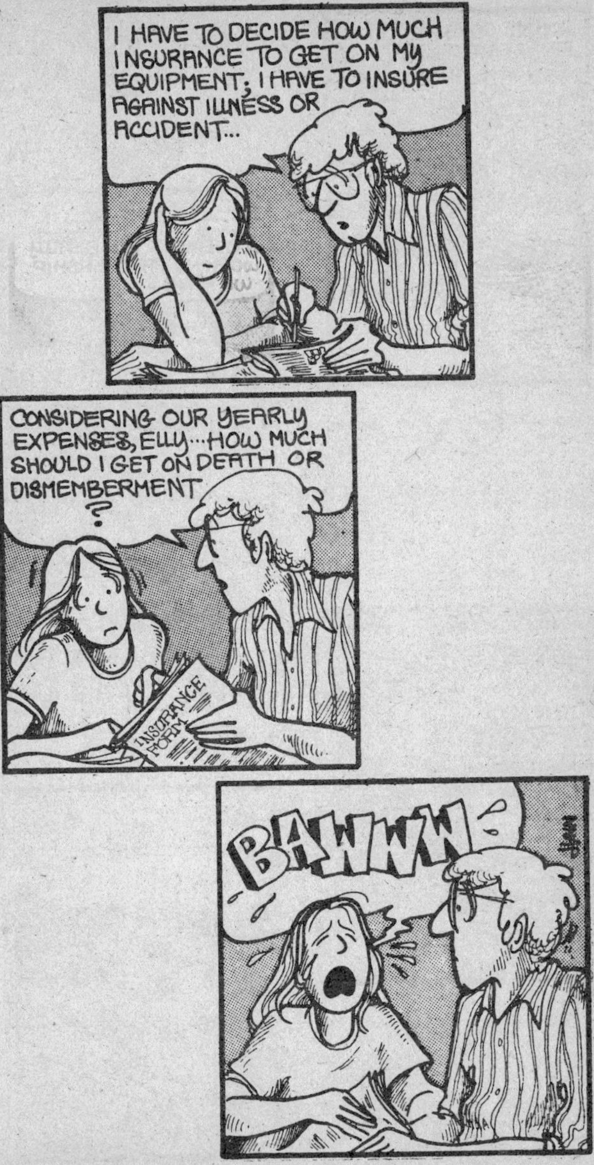
I HAVE TO DECIDE HOW MUCH INSURANCE TO GET ON MY EQUIPMENT; I HAVE TO INSURE AGAINST ILLNESS OR ACCIDENT...
CONSIDERING OUR YEARLY EXPENSES, ELLY...HOW MUCH SHOULD I GET ON DEATH OR DISMEMBERMENT?
INSURANCE FORM
BAWWW

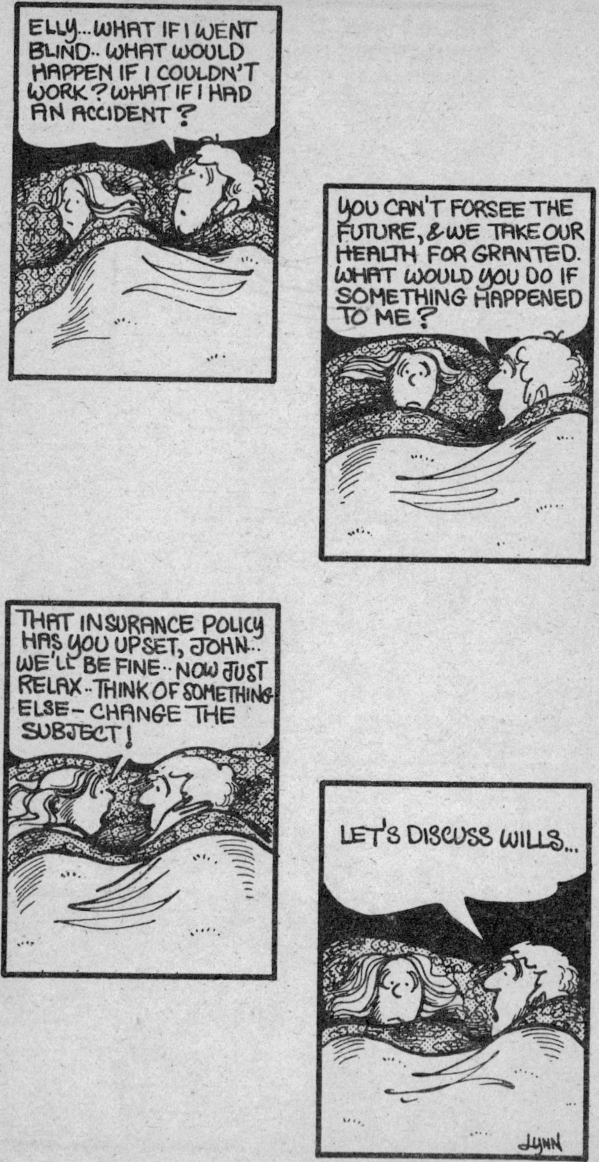
ELLY...WHAT IF I WENT BLIND.. WHAT WOULD HAPPEN IF I COULDN'T WORK? WHAT IF I HAD AN ACCIDENT?
YOU CAN'T FORSEE THE FUTURE, & WE TAKE OUR HEALTH FOR GRANTED. WHAT WOULD YOU DO IF SOMETHING HAPPENED TO ME?
THAT INSURANCE POLICY HAS YOU UPSET, JOHN.. WE'LL BE FINE.. NOW JUST RELAX.. THINK OF SOMETHING ELSE – CHANGE THE SUBJECT!
LET'S DISCUSS WILLS...
LYNN

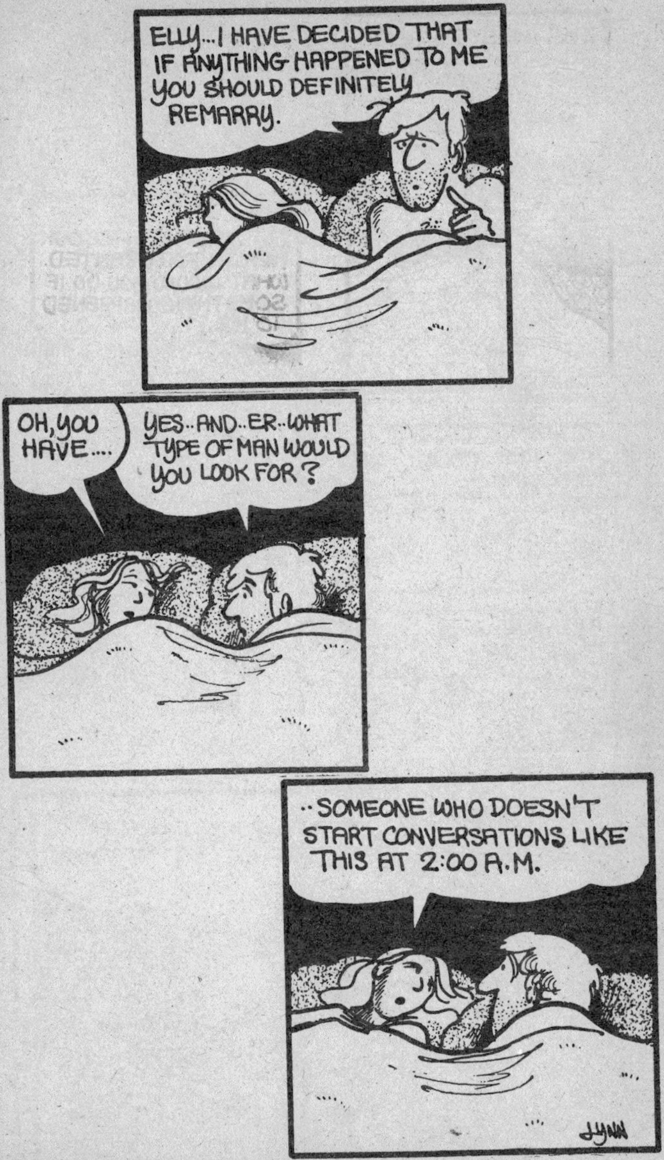
ELLY...I HAVE DECIDED THAT IF ANYTHING HAPPENED TO ME YOU SHOULD DEFINITELY REMARRY.
OH, YOU HAVE....
YES..AND..ER..WHAT TYPE OF MAN WOULD YOU LOOK FOR?
..SOMEONE WHO DOESN'T START CONVERSATIONS LIKE THIS AT 2:00 A.M.
LYNN

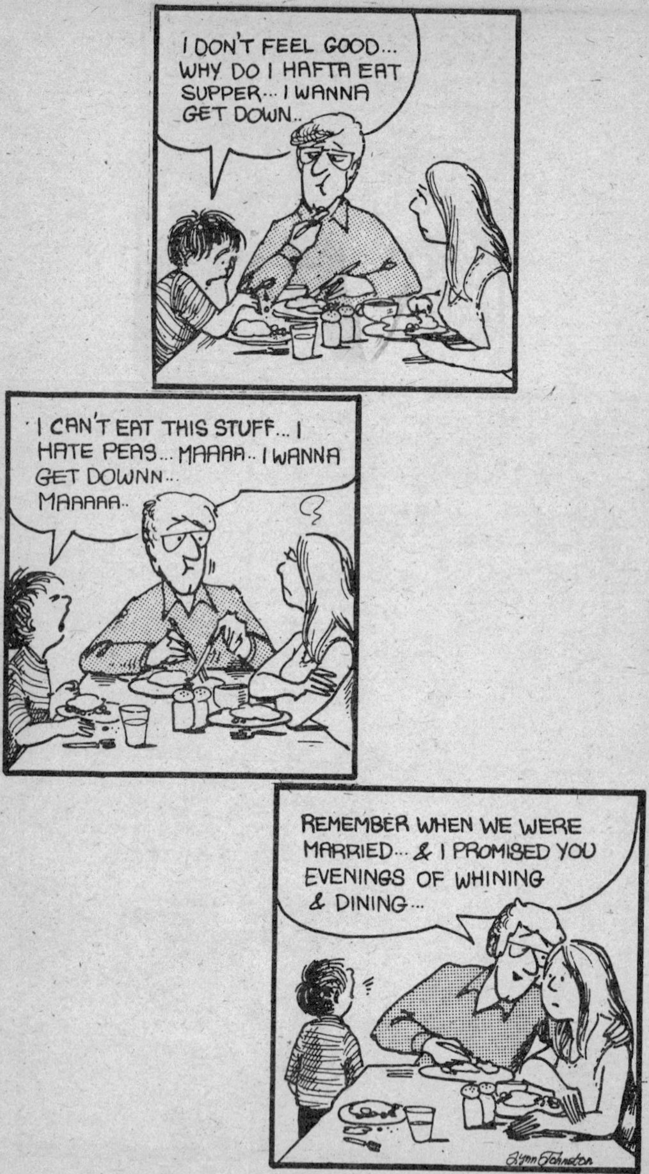
I DON'T FEEL GOOD... WHY DO I HAFTA EAT SUPPER... I WANNA GET DOWN..
I CAN'T EAT THIS STUFF... I HATE PEAS... MAAAA.. I WANNA GET DOWNN... MAAAAA..
REMEMBER WHEN WE WERE MARRIED... & I PROMISED YOU EVENINGS OF WHINING & DINING...
Lynn Johnston

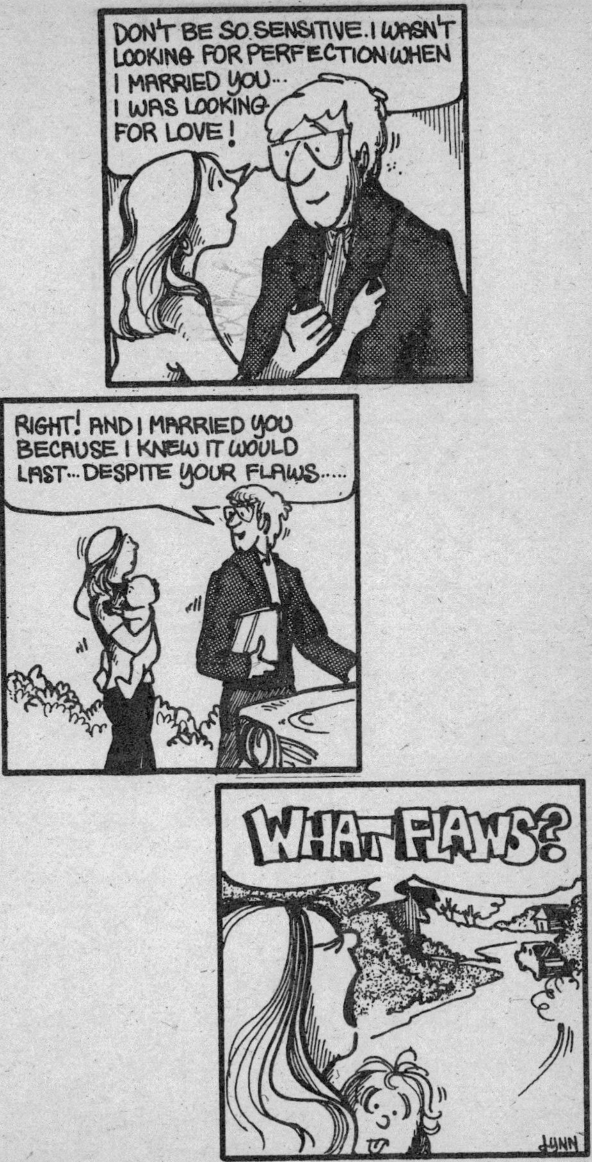
DON'T BE SO SENSITIVE. I WASN'T LOOKING FOR PERFECTION WHEN I MARRIED YOU... I WAS LOOKING FOR LOVE!
RIGHT! AND I MARRIED YOU BECAUSE I KNEW IT WOULD LAST... DESPITE YOUR FLAWS.....
WHAT FLAWS?
LYNN

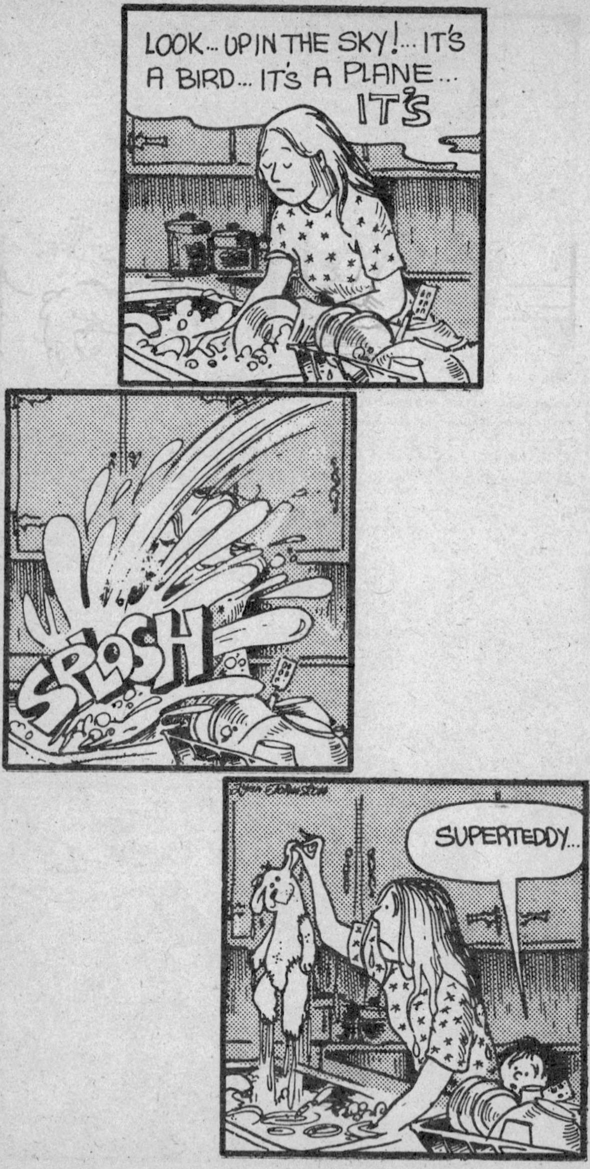
LOOK... UP IN THE SKY!... IT'S A BIRD... IT'S A PLANE...
IT'S
SPLOSH
SUPERTEDDY...

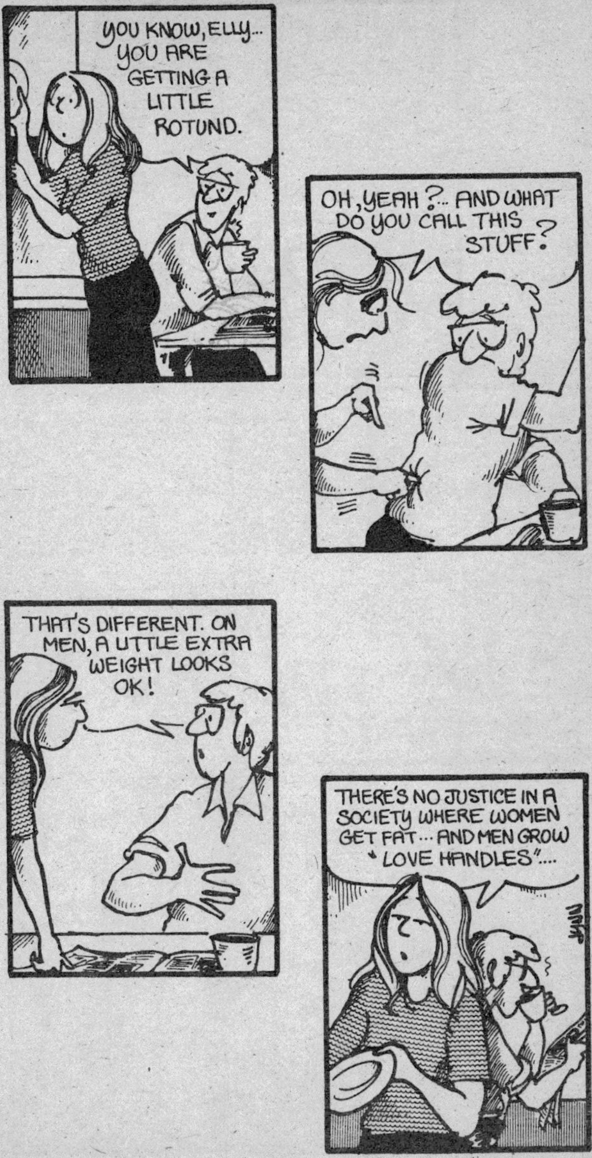
YOU KNOW, ELLY... YOU ARE GETTING A LITTLE ROTUND.
OH, YEAH?... AND WHAT DO YOU CALL THIS STUFF?
THAT'S DIFFERENT. ON MEN, A LITTLE EXTRA WEIGHT LOOKS OK!
THERE'S NO JUSTICE IN A SOCIETY WHERE WOMEN GET FAT... AND MEN GROW "LOVE HANDLES"....

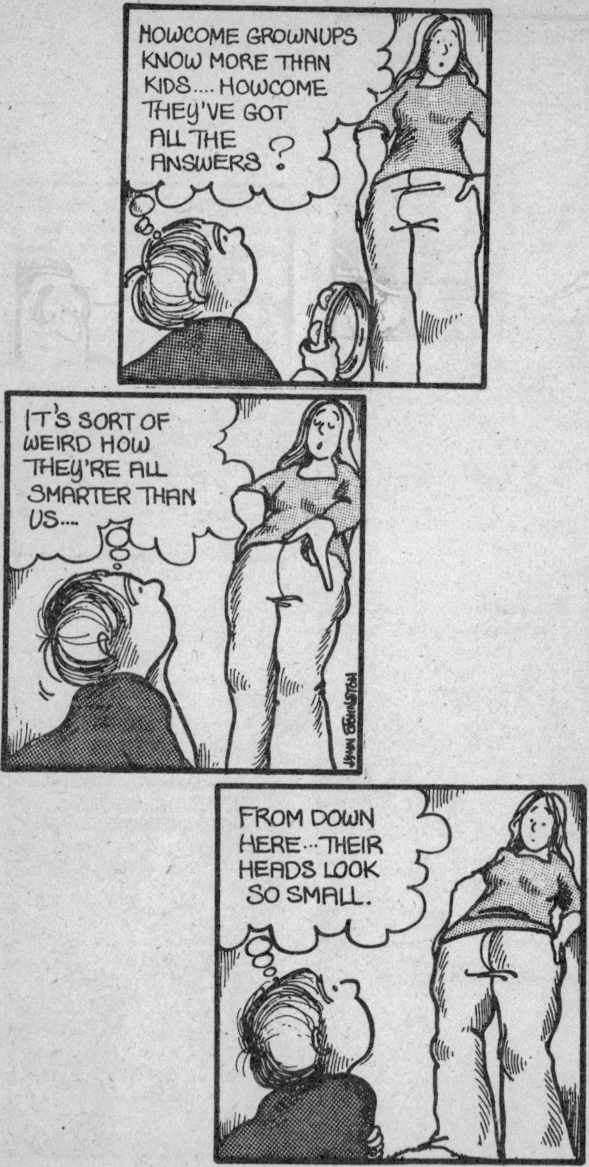
HOWCOME GROWNUPS KNOW MORE THAN KIDS.... HOWCOME THEY'VE GOT ALL THE ANSWERS?
IT'S SORT OF WEIRD HOW THEY'RE ALL SMARTER THAN US....
FROM DOWN HERE... THEIR HEADS LOOK SO SMALL.

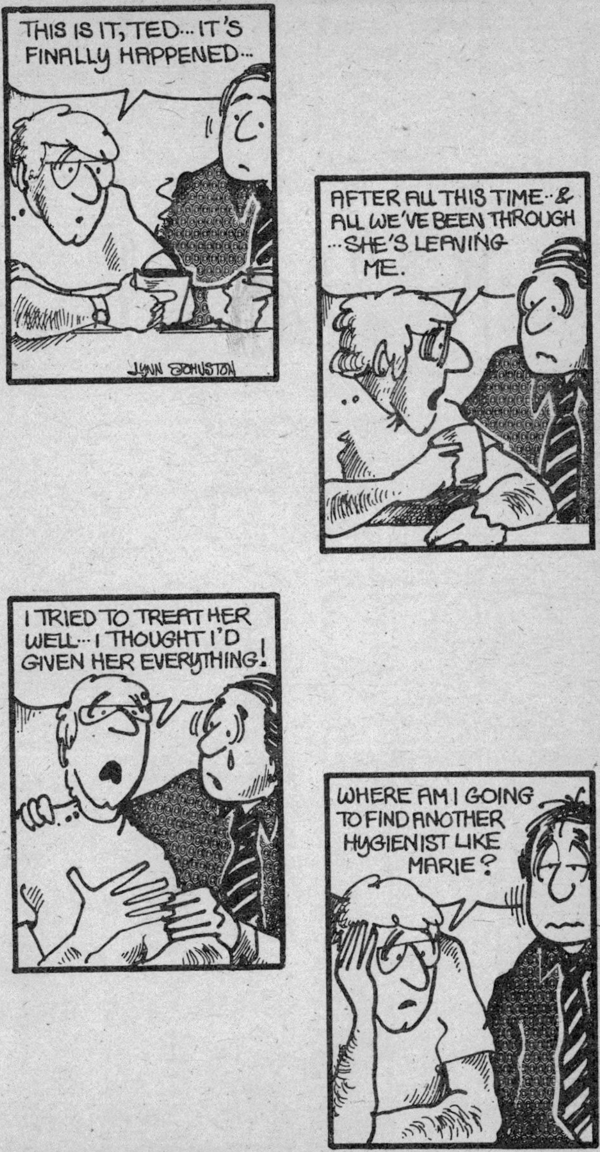
THIS IS IT, TED... IT'S FINALLY HAPPENED...
LYNN JOHNSTON
AFTER ALL THIS TIME..& ALL WE'VE BEEN THROUGH ...SHE'S LEAVING ME.
I TRIED TO TREAT HER WELL... I THOUGHT I'D GIVEN HER EVERYTHING!
WHERE AM I GOING TO FIND ANOTHER HYGIENIST LIKE MARIE?

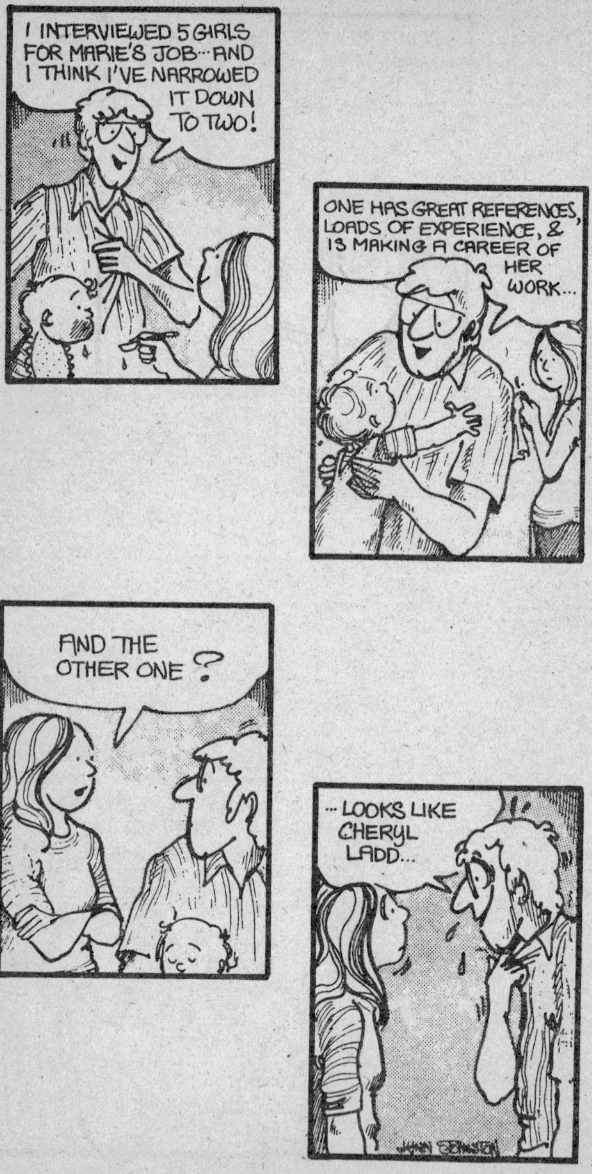
I INTERVIEWED 5 GIRLS FOR MARIE'S JOB... AND I THINK I'VE NARROWED IT DOWN TO TWO!
ONE HAS GREAT REFERENCES, LOADS OF EXPERIENCE, & IS MAKING A CAREER OF HER WORK...
AND THE OTHER ONE?
...LOOKS LIKE CHERYL LADD...
LYNN JOHNSTON

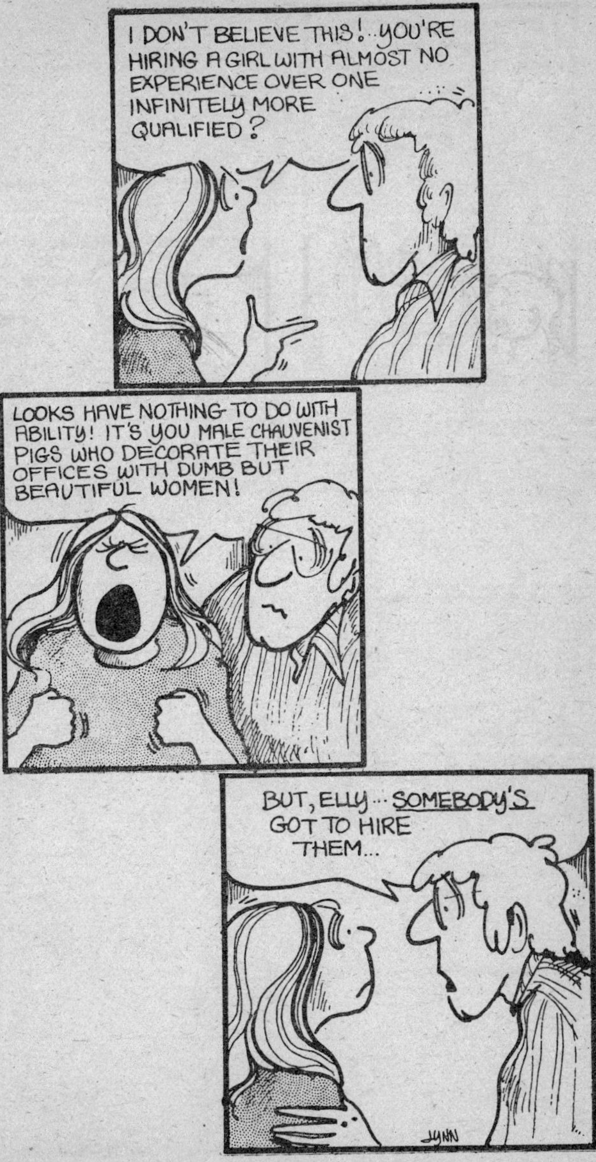
I DON'T BELIEVE THIS!...YOU'RE HIRING A GIRL WITH ALMOST NO EXPERIENCE OVER ONE INFINITELY MORE QUALIFIED?
LOOKS HAVE NOTHING TO DO WITH ABILITY! IT'S YOU MALE CHAUVENIST PIGS WHO DECORATE THEIR OFFICES WITH DUMB BUT BEAUTIFUL WOMEN!
BUT, ELLY... SOMEBODY'S GOT TO HIRE THEM...
LYNN

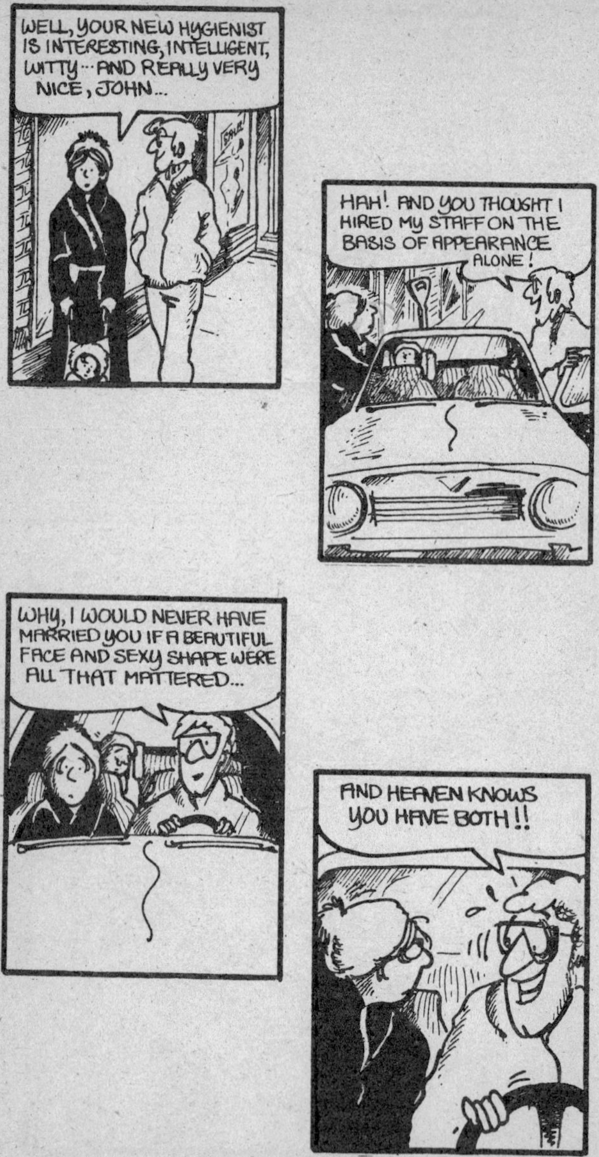
WELL, YOUR NEW HYGIENIST IS INTERESTING, INTELLIGENT, WITTY ··· AND REALLY VERY NICE, JOHN...
HAH! AND YOU THOUGHT I HIRED MY STAFF ON THE BASIS OF APPEARANCE ALONE!
WHY, I WOULD NEVER HAVE MARRIED YOU IF A BEAUTIFUL FACE AND SEXY SHAPE WERE ALL THAT MATTERED...
AND HEAVEN KNOWS YOU HAVE BOTH!!

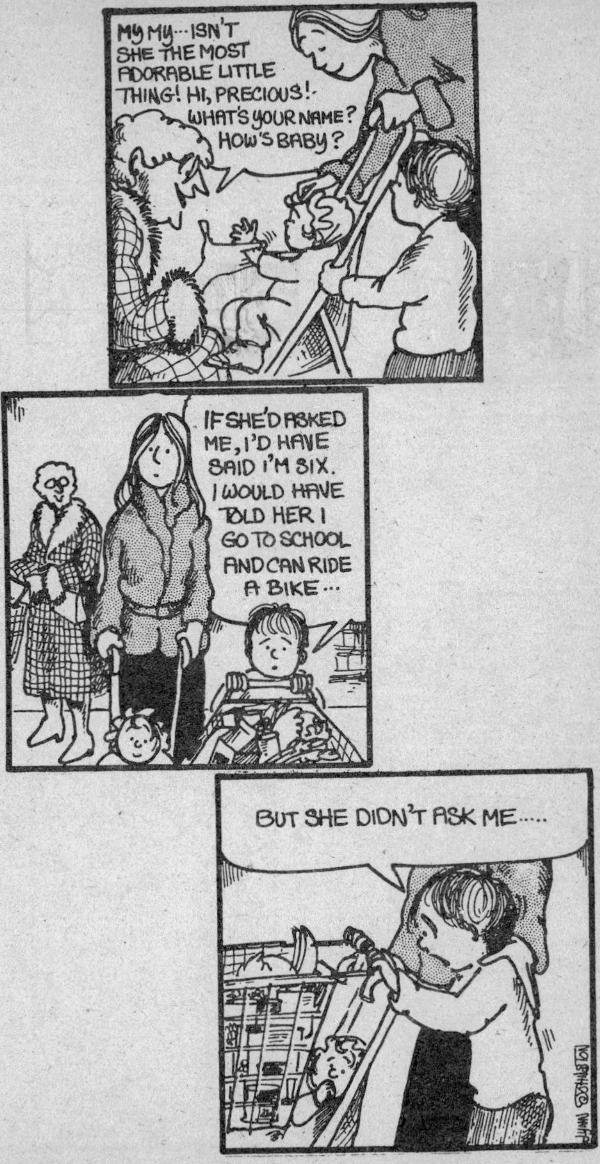
MY MY…ISN'T SHE THE MOST ADORABLE LITTLE THING! HI, PRECIOUS!
WHAT'S YOUR NAME?
HOW'S BABY?
IF SHE'D ASKED ME, I'D HAVE SAID I'M SIX. I WOULD HAVE TOLD HER I GO TO SCHOOL AND CAN RIDE A BIKE…
BUT SHE DIDN'T ASK ME…..

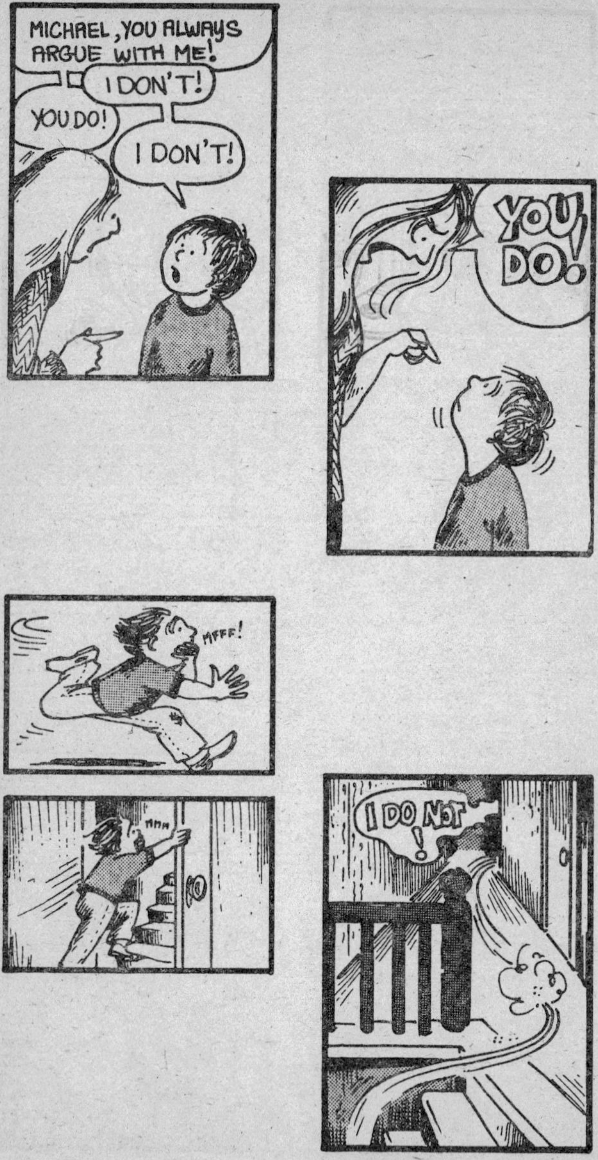

MICHAEL, YOU ALWAYS ARGUE WITH ME!
I DON'T!
YOU DO!
I DON'T!
YOU DO!
MFFF!
MMM
I DO NOT!

GLAH?
BLFF!
DOO?
I'D BETTER GO, MOM... ELIZABETH IS BEING TOO QUIET.

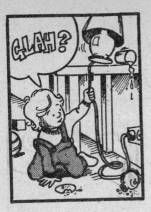

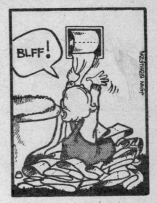

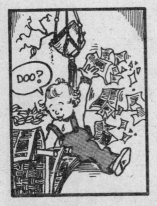

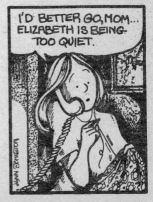

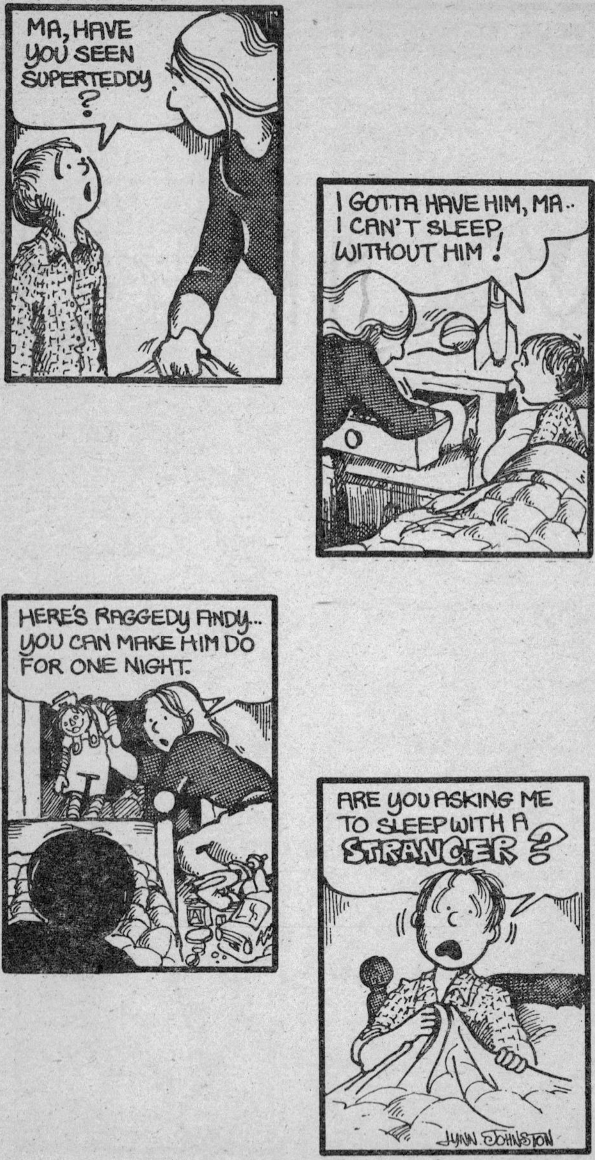
MA, HAVE YOU SEEN SUPERTEDDY?
I GOTTA HAVE HIM, MA.. I CAN'T SLEEP WITHOUT HIM!
HERE'S RAGGEDY ANDY... YOU CAN MAKE HIM DO FOR ONE NIGHT.
ARE YOU ASKING ME TO SLEEP WITH A STRANGER?
LYNN JOHNSTON

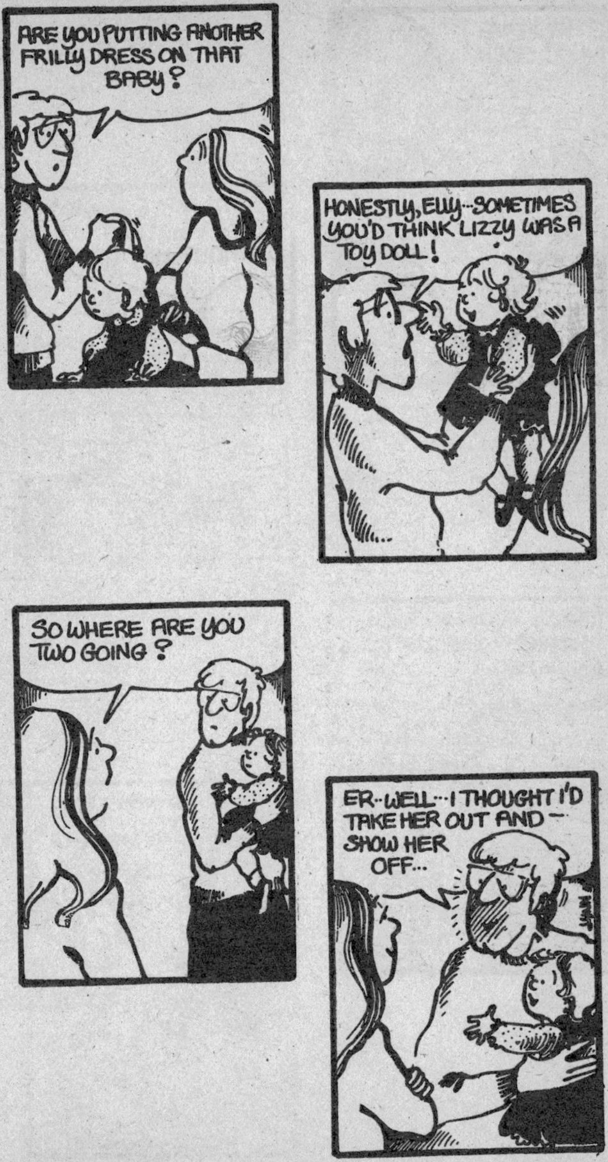
ARE YOU PUTTING ANOTHER FRILLY DRESS ON THAT BABY?
HONESTLY, ELLY...SOMETIMES YOU'D THINK LIZZY WAS A TOY DOLL!
SO WHERE ARE YOU TWO GOING?
ER...WELL...I THOUGHT I'D TAKE HER OUT AND — SHOW HER OFF...

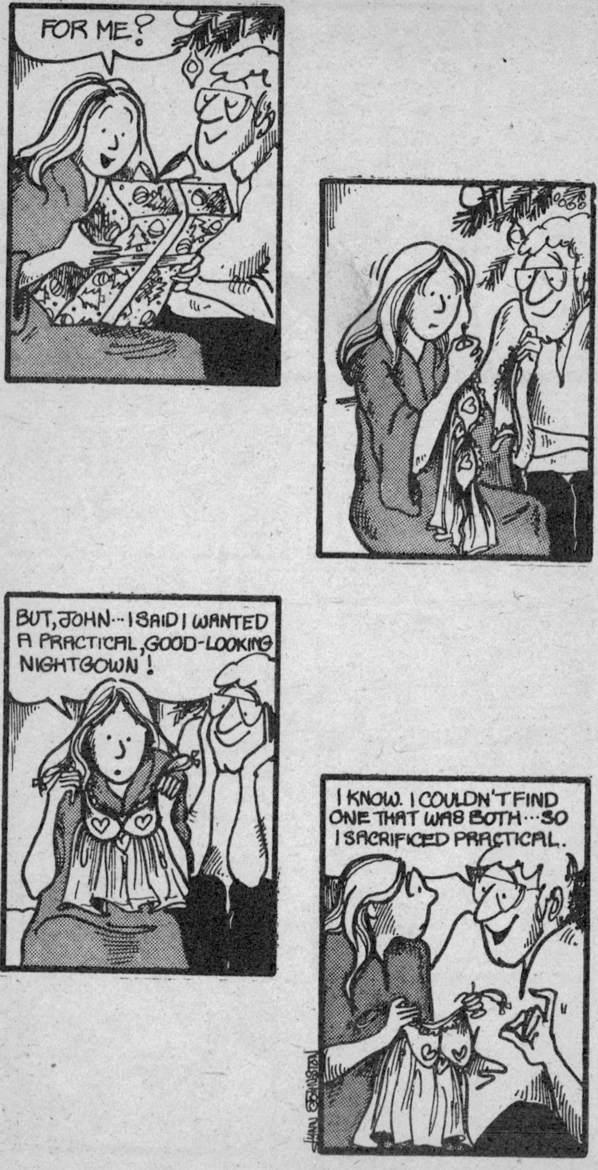
FOR ME?
BUT, JOHN··· I SAID I WANTED A PRACTICAL, GOOD-LOOKING NIGHTGOWN!
I KNOW. I COULDN'T FIND ONE THAT WAS BOTH··· SO I SACRIFICED PRACTICAL.

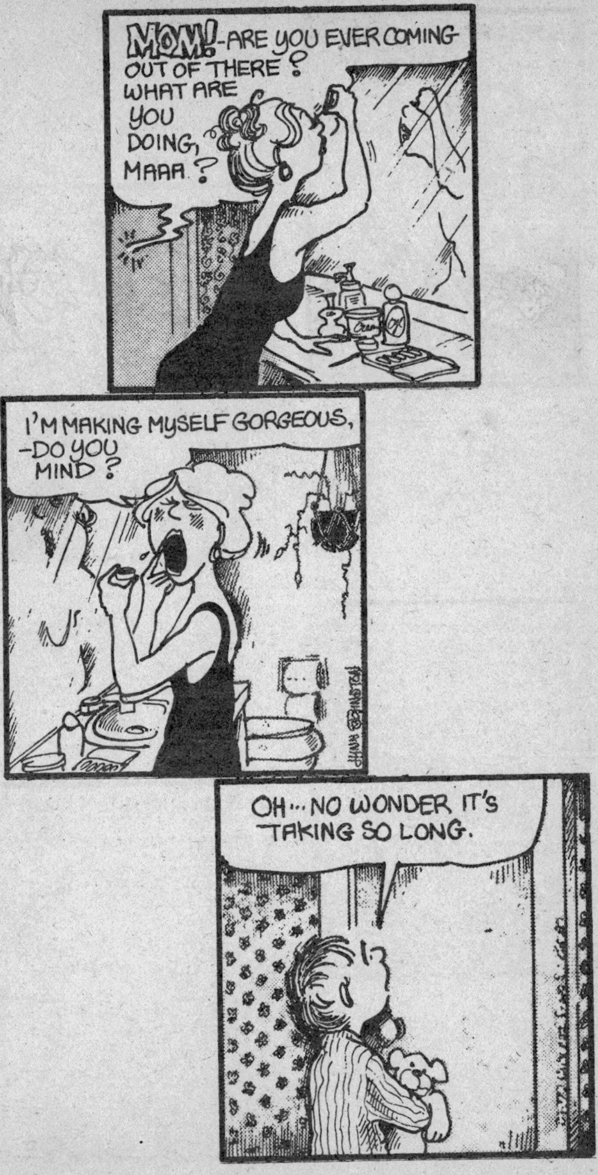
MOM!-ARE YOU EVER COMING OUT OF THERE? WHAT ARE YOU DOING, MAAA?
I'M MAKING MYSELF GORGEOUS, -DO YOU MIND?
OH... NO WONDER IT'S TAKING SO LONG.

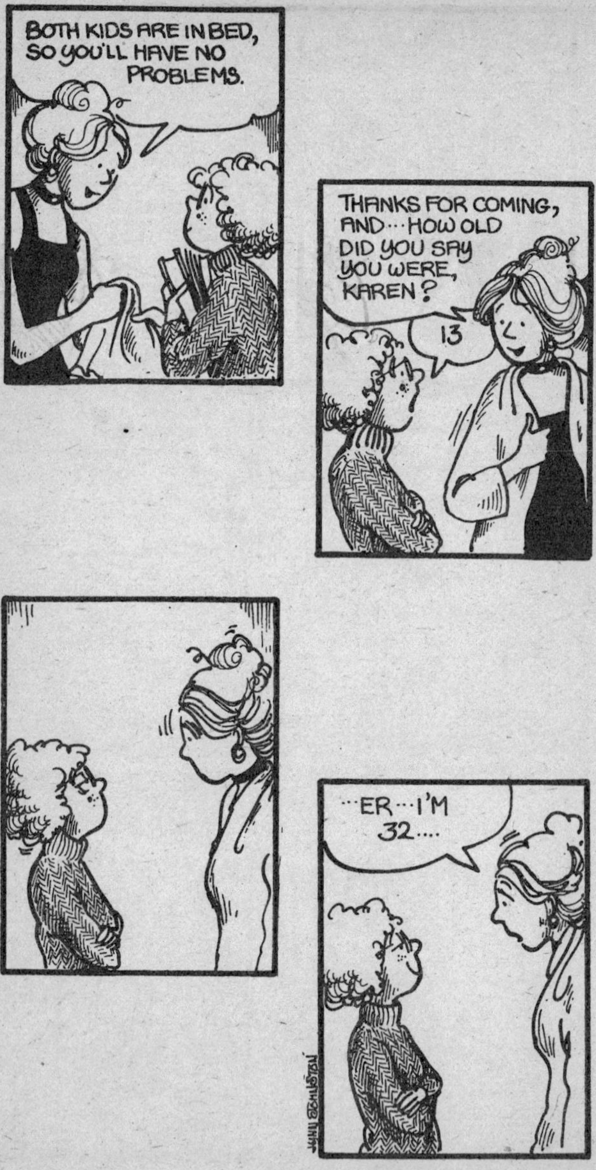
BOTH KIDS ARE IN BED, SO YOU'LL HAVE NO PROBLEMS.
THANKS FOR COMING, AND··· HOW OLD DID YOU SAY YOU WERE, KAREN?
13
···ER···I'M 32....
LYNN JOHNSTON

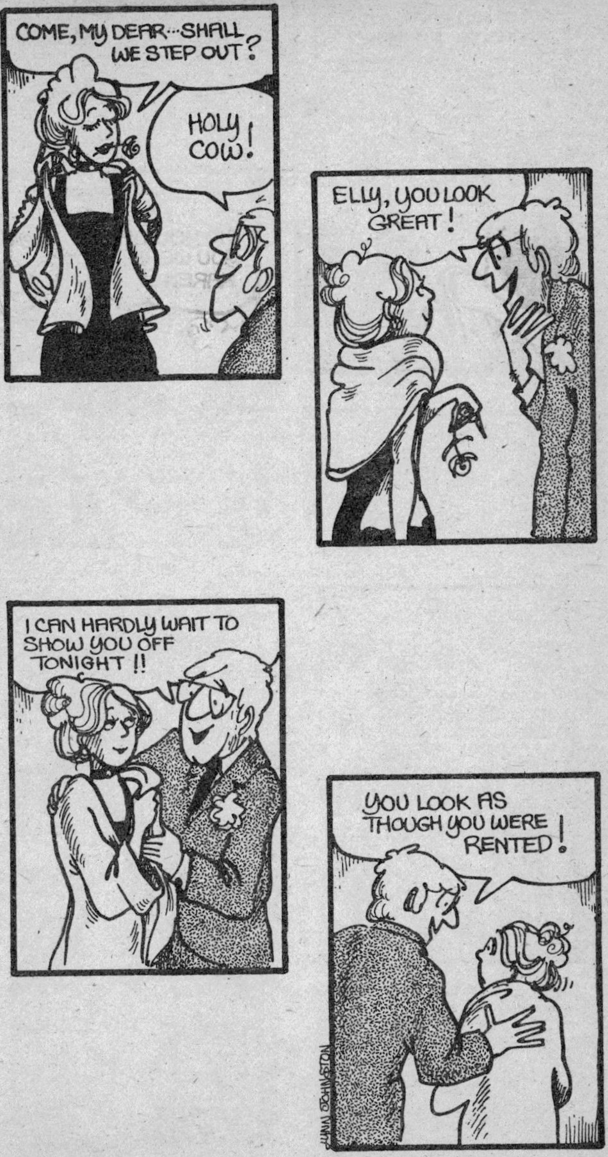
COME, MY DEAR···SHALL WE STEP OUT?
HOLY COW!
ELLY, YOU LOOK GREAT!
I CAN HARDLY WAIT TO SHOW YOU OFF TONIGHT!!
YOU LOOK AS THOUGH YOU WERE RENTED!
LYNN JOHNSTON

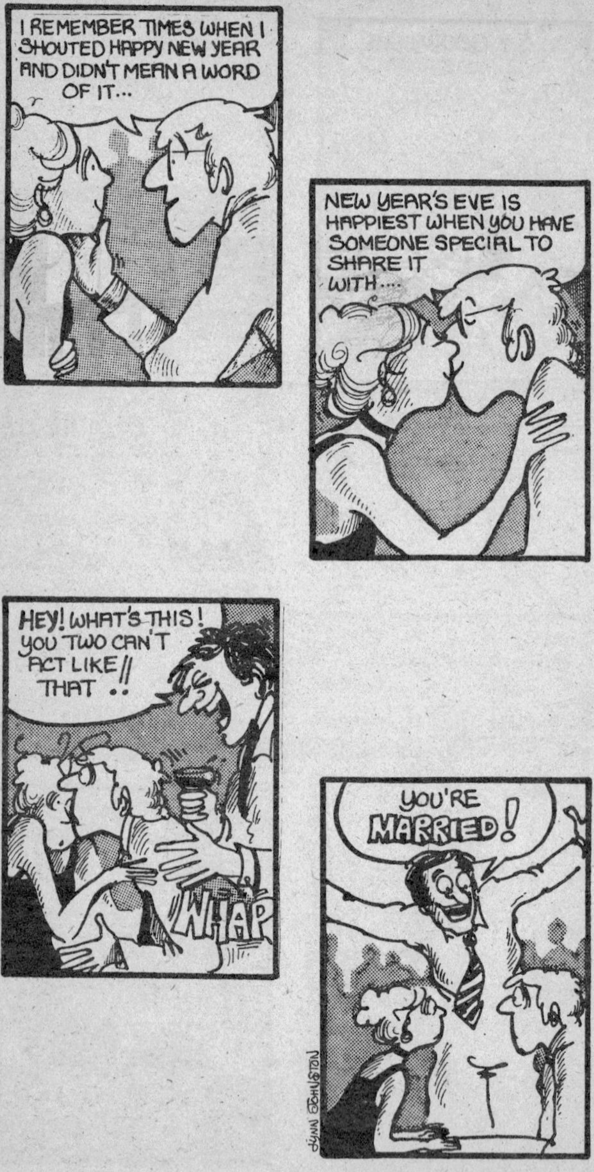
I REMEMBER TIMES WHEN I SHOUTED HAPPY NEW YEAR AND DIDN'T MEAN A WORD OF IT...
NEW YEAR'S EVE IS HAPPIEST WHEN YOU HAVE SOMEONE SPECIAL TO SHARE IT WITH....
HEY! WHAT'S THIS! YOU TWO CAN'T ACT LIKE THAT!!
WHAP
YOU'RE MARRIED!
LYNN JOHNSTON

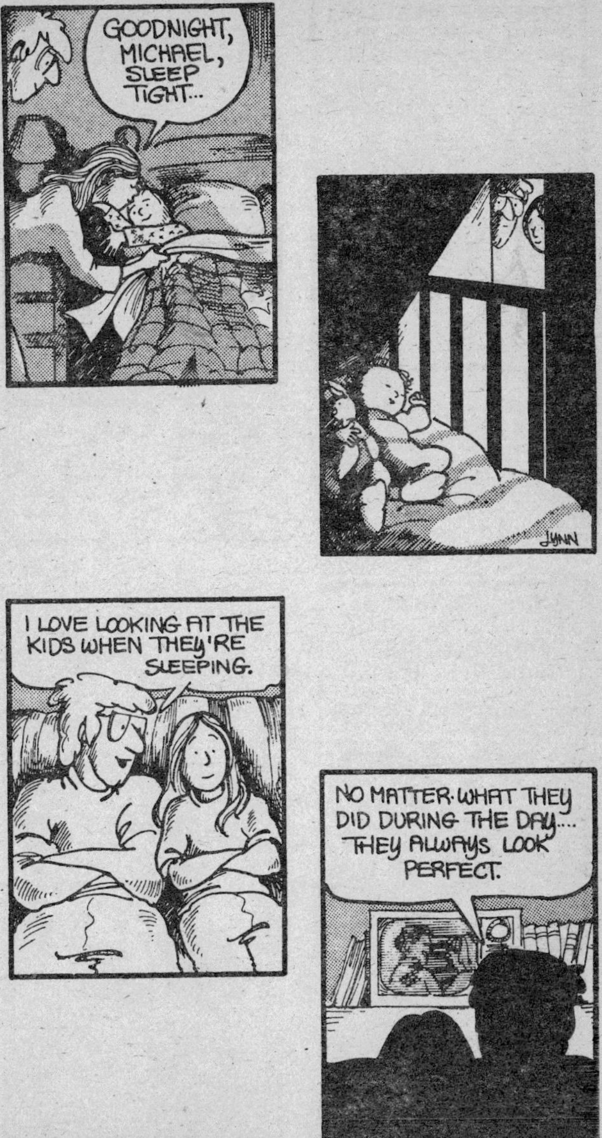
GOODNIGHT, MICHAEL, SLEEP TIGHT...
LYNN
I LOVE LOOKING AT THE KIDS WHEN THEY'RE SLEEPING.
NO MATTER WHAT THEY DID DURING THE DAY.... THEY ALWAYS LOOK PERFECT.

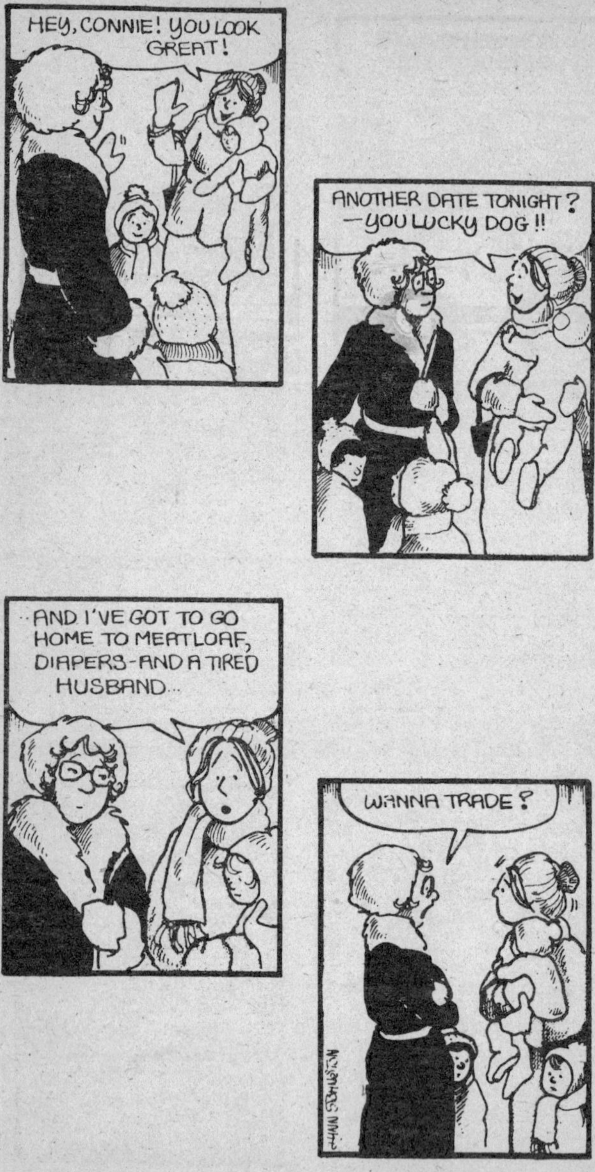
HEY, CONNIE! YOU LOOK GREAT!
ANOTHER DATE TONIGHT? —YOU LUCKY DOG!!
..AND I'VE GOT TO GO HOME TO MEATLOAF, DIAPERS - AND A TIRED HUSBAND...
WANNA TRADE?
LYNN JOHNSTON

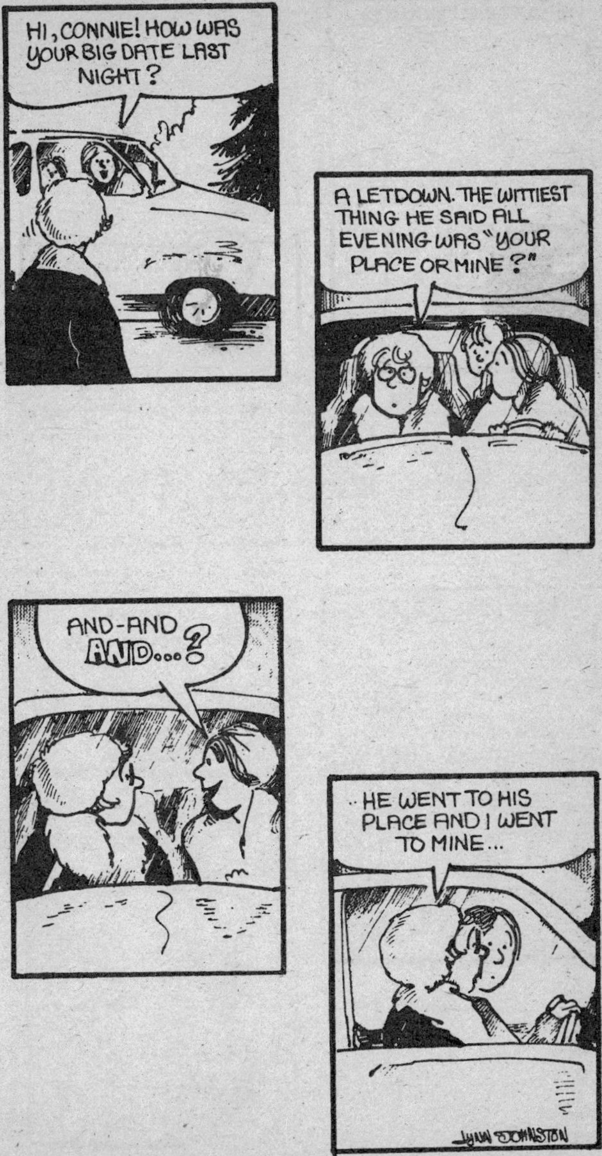
HI, CONNIE! HOW WAS YOUR BIG DATE LAST NIGHT?
A LETDOWN. THE WITTIEST THING HE SAID ALL EVENING WAS "YOUR PLACE OR MINE?"
AND-AND AND...?
..HE WENT TO HIS PLACE AND I WENT TO MINE...
LYNN JOHNSTON

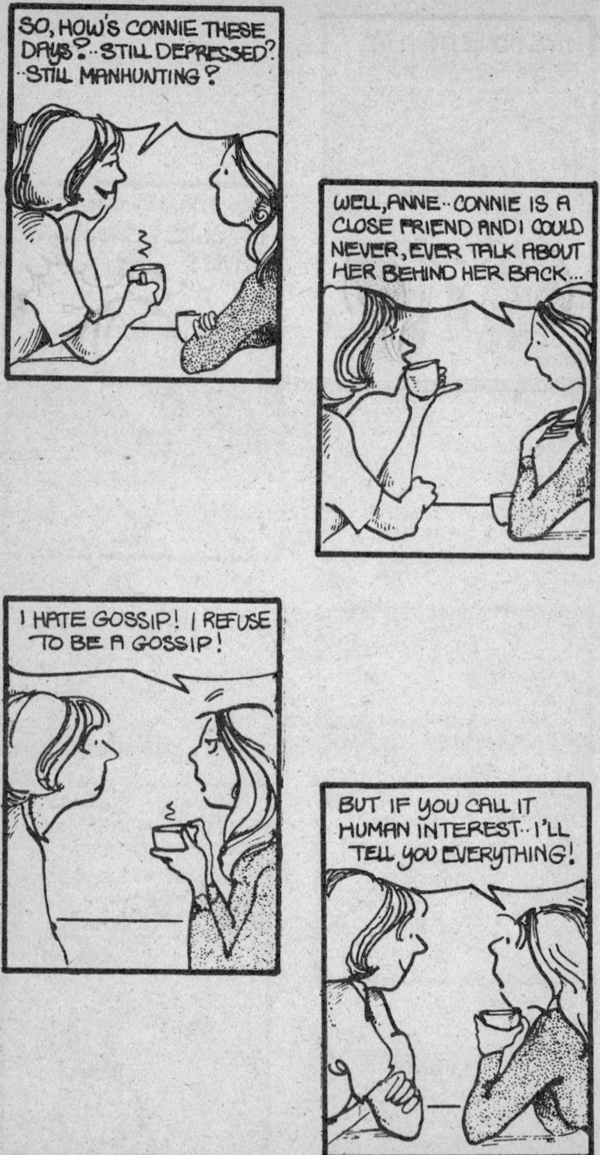
SO, HOW'S CONNIE THESE DAYS?..STILL DEPRESSED? ..STILL MANHUNTING?
WELL, ANNE.. CONNIE IS A CLOSE FRIEND AND I COULD NEVER, EVER TALK ABOUT HER BEHIND HER BACK...
I HATE GOSSIP! I REFUSE TO BE A GOSSIP!
BUT IF YOU CALL IT HUMAN INTEREST.. I'LL TELL YOU EVERYTHING!

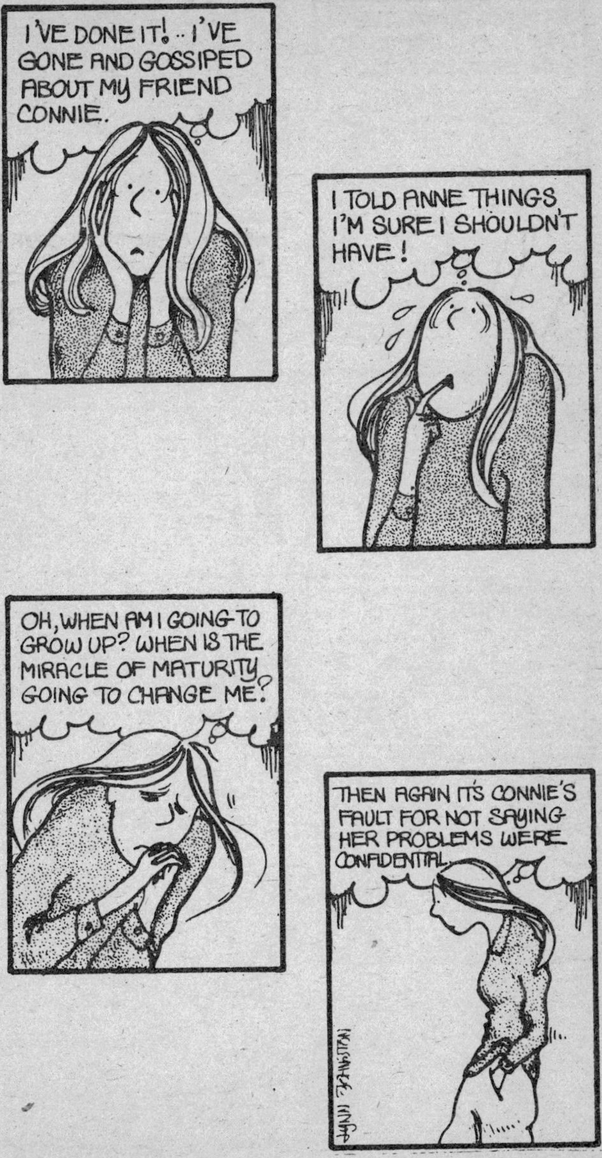
I'VE DONE IT! .. I'VE GONE AND GOSSIPED ABOUT MY FRIEND CONNIE.
I TOLD ANNE THINGS I'M SURE I SHOULDN'T HAVE!
OH, WHEN AM I GOING TO GROW UP? WHEN IS THE MIRACLE OF MATURITY GOING TO CHANGE ME?
THEN AGAIN IT'S CONNIE'S FAULT FOR NOT SAYING HER PROBLEMS WERE CONFIDENTIAL.

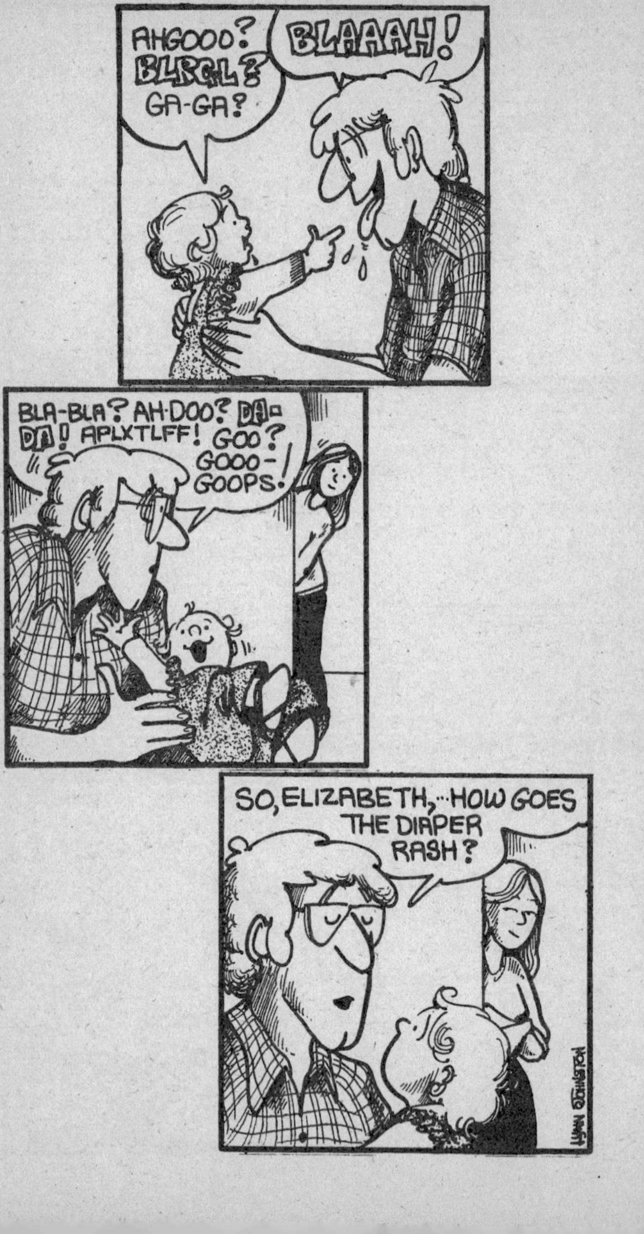
AHGOOO? BLRGL? GA-GA?
BLAAAH!
BLA-BLA? AH-DOO? DA-DA! APLXTLFF! GOO? GOOO-GOOPS!
SO, ELIZABETH,...HOW GOES THE DIAPER RASH?
LYNN JOHNSTON

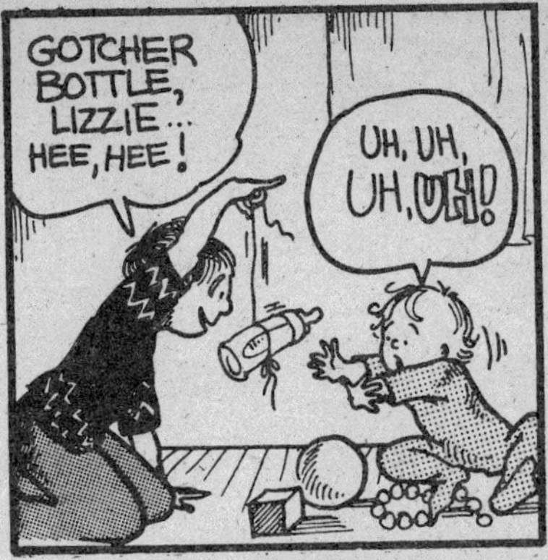
GOTCHER BOTTLE, LIZZIE... HEE, HEE!
UH, UH, UH, UH!

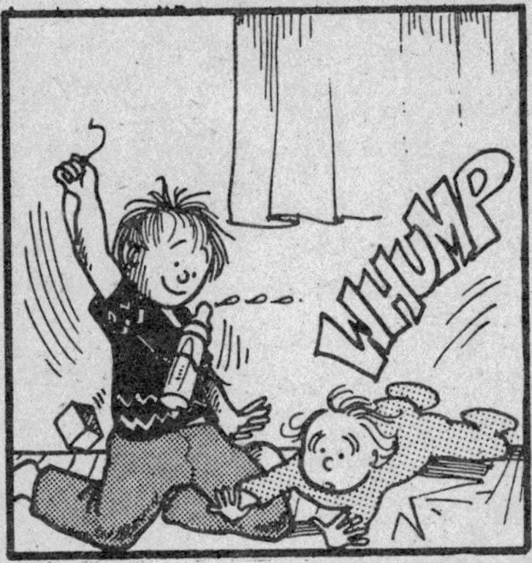
WHUMP

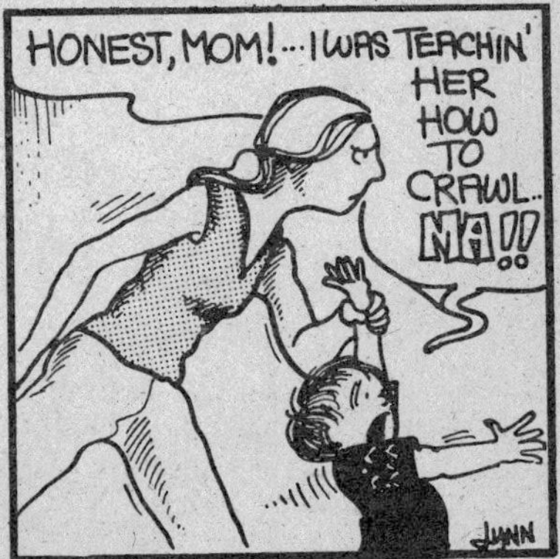
HONEST, MOM!... I WAS TEACHIN' HER HOW TO CRAWL.. NA!!
LYNN

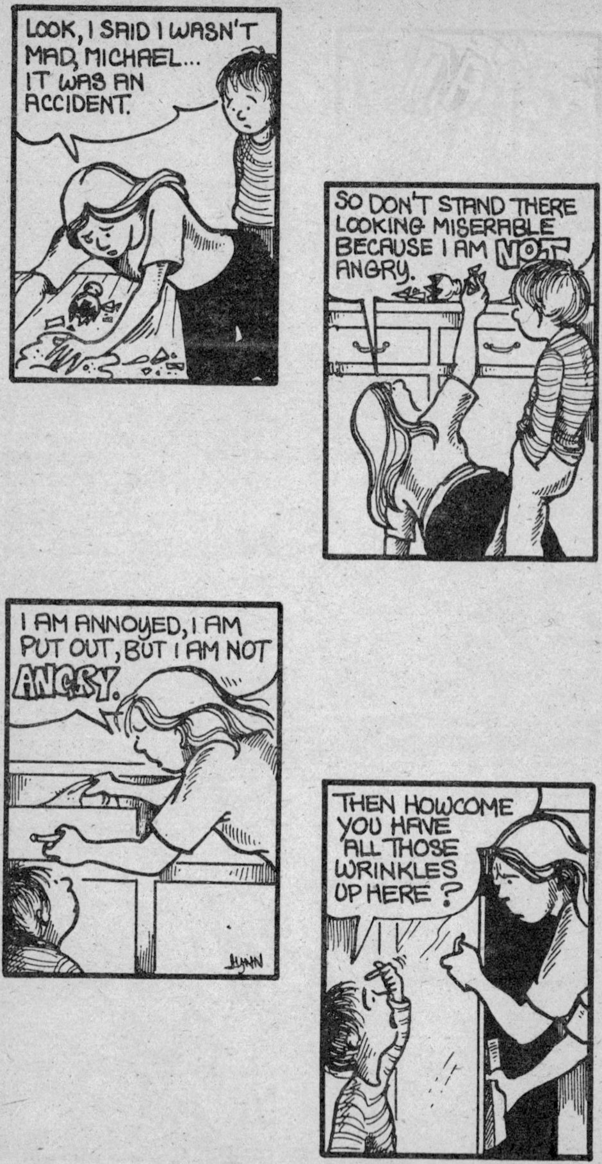
LOOK, I SAID I WASN'T MAD, MICHAEL... IT WAS AN ACCIDENT.
SO DON'T STAND THERE LOOKING MISERABLE BECAUSE I AM NOT ANGRY.
I AM ANNOYED, I AM PUT OUT, BUT I AM NOT ANGRY.
LYNN
THEN HOWCOME YOU HAVE ALL THOSE WRINKLES UP HERE?

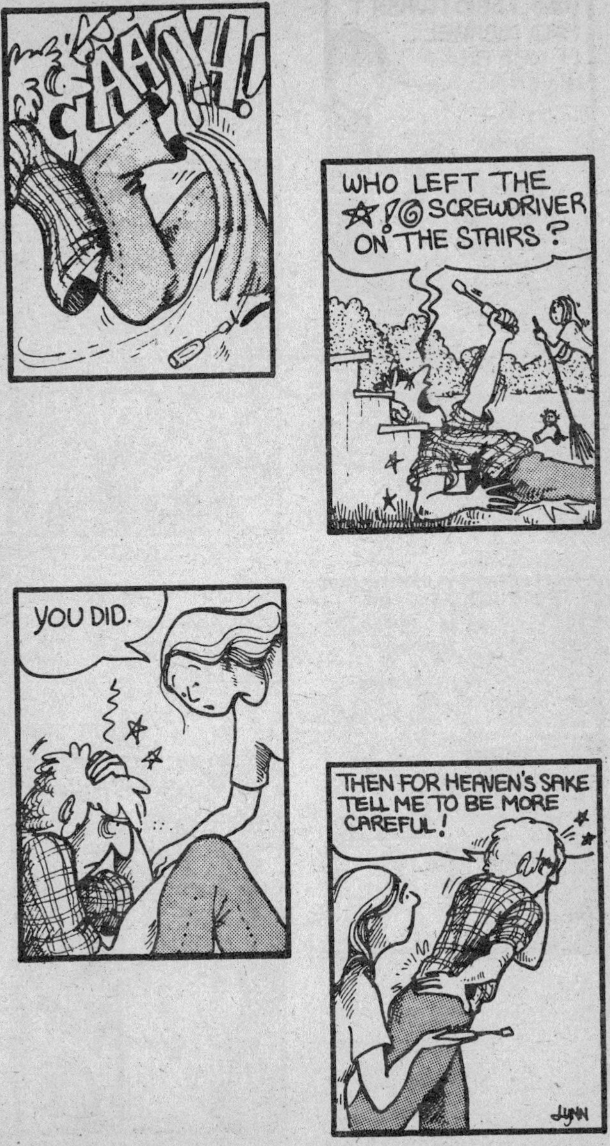

WHO LEFT THE ☆!@ SCREWDRIVER ON THE STAIRS?
YOU DID.
THEN FOR HEAVEN'S SAKE TELL ME TO BE MORE CAREFUL!
LYNN

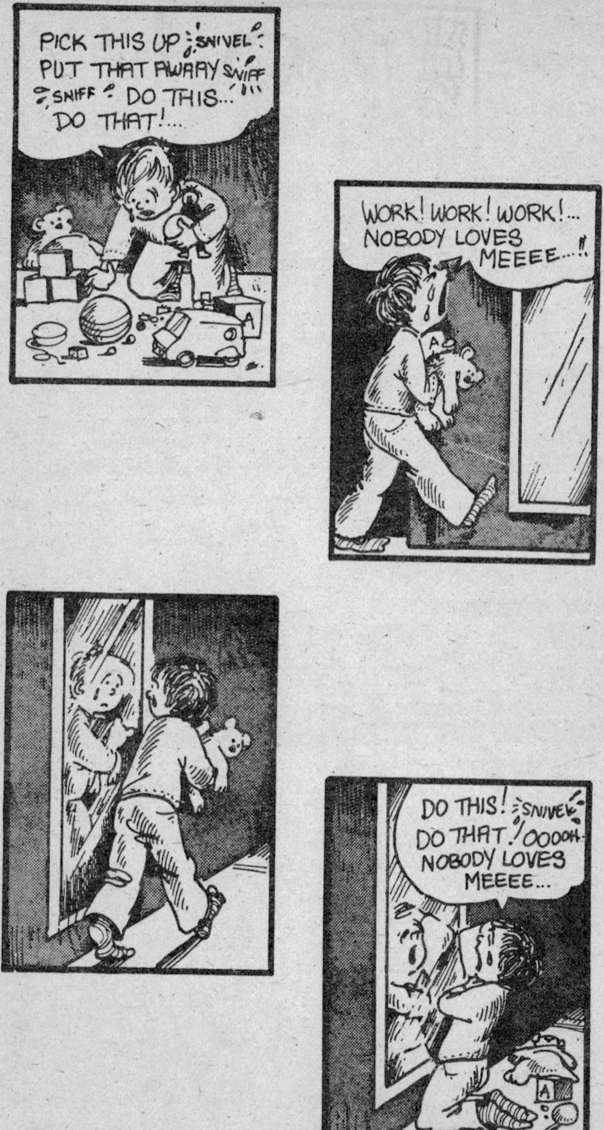
PICK THIS UP SNIVEL PUT THAT AWAAY SNIFF SNIFF DO THIS... DO THAT!...
WORK! WORK! WORK!... NOBODY LOVES MEEEE...!!
DO THIS! SNIVEL DO THAT! OOOOH NOBODY LOVES MEEEE...
Lynn Johnston

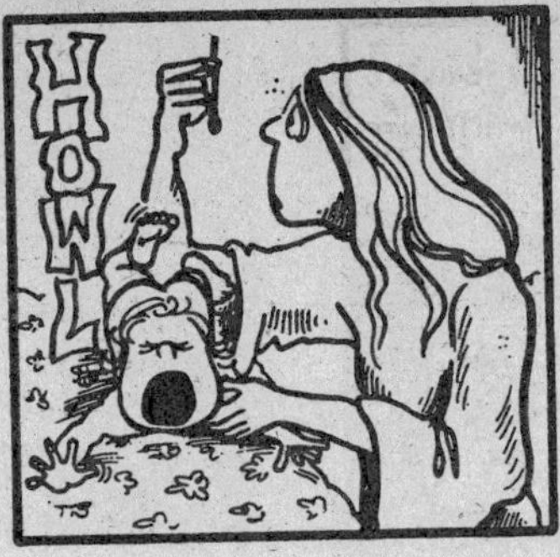
HOWL

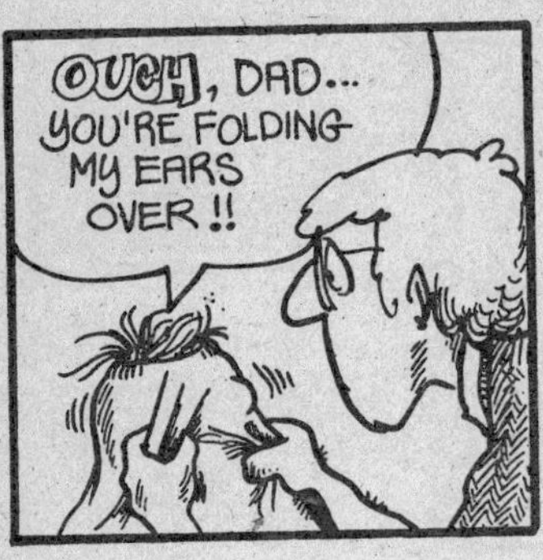
OUCH, DAD...
YOU'RE FOLDING MY EARS OVER !!

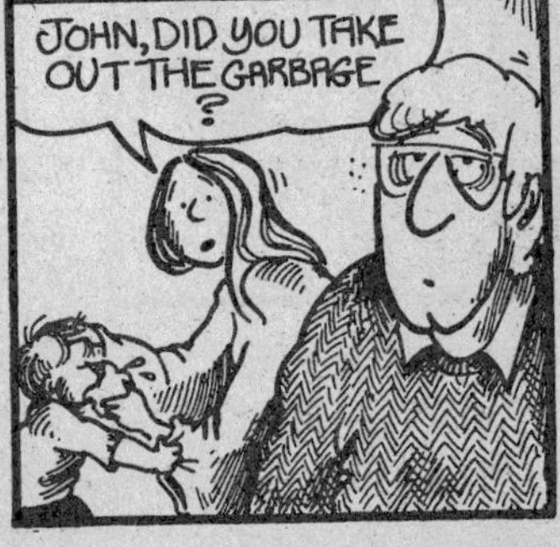
JOHN, DID YOU TAKE OUT THE GARBAGE ?

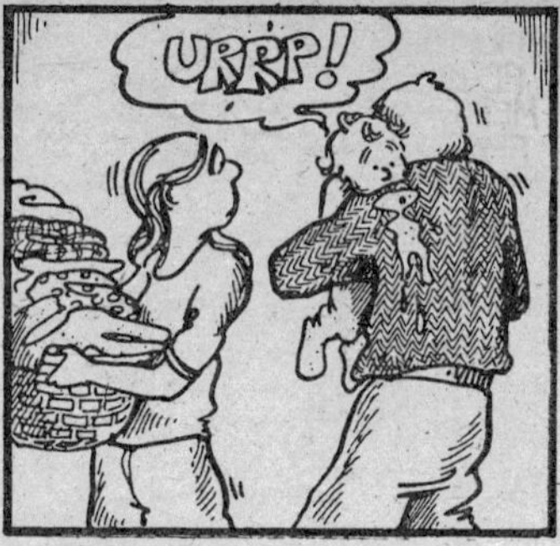
URRP!

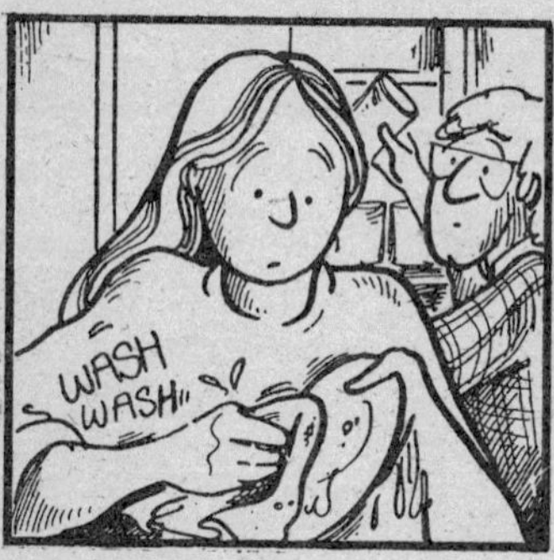
WASH WASH

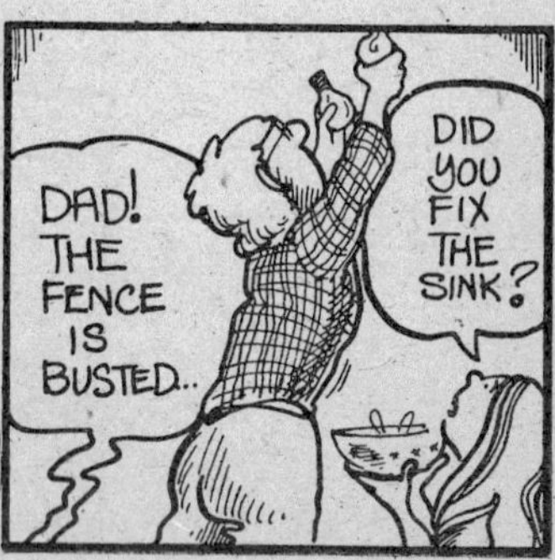
DAD! THE FENCE IS BUSTED..
DID YOU FIX THE SINK?

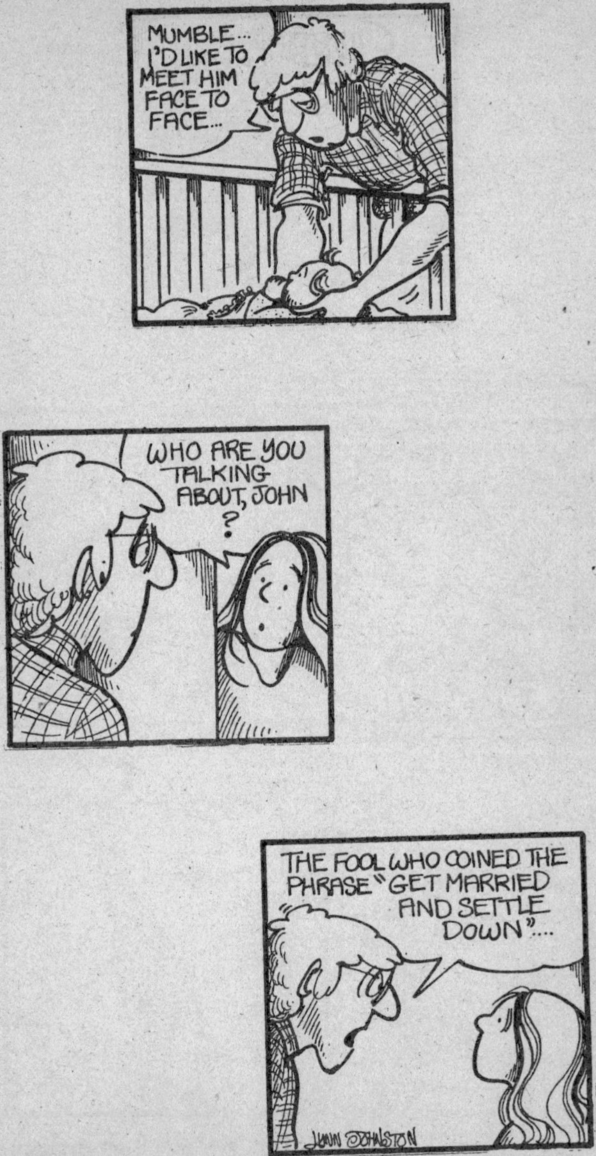
MUMBLE... I'D LIKE TO MEET HIM FACE TO FACE...
WHO ARE YOU TALKING ABOUT, JOHN ?
THE FOOL WHO COINED THE PHRASE "GET MARRIED AND SETTLE DOWN"....
LYNN JOHNSTON

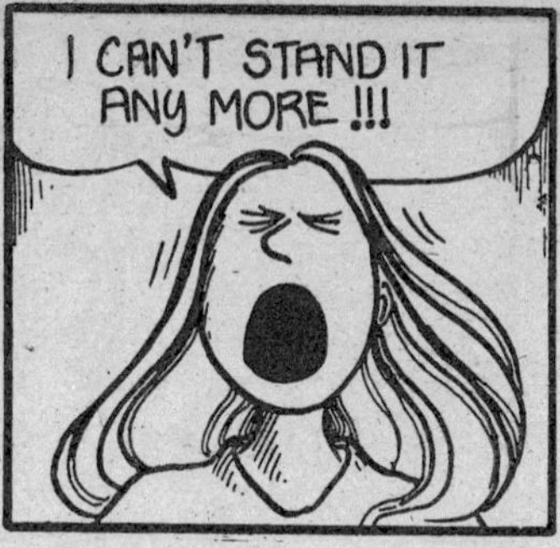
I CAN'T STAND IT ANY MORE !!!

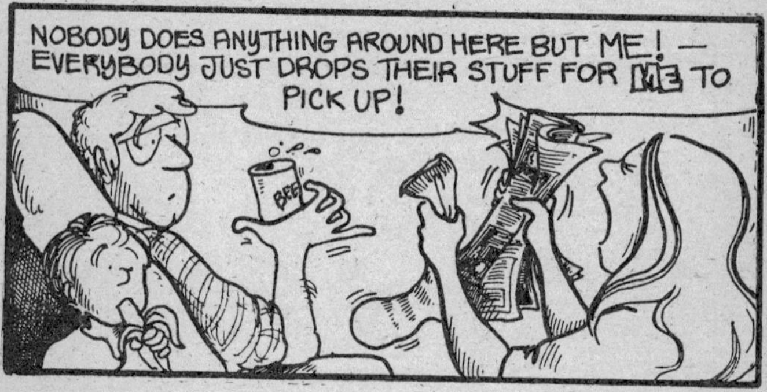
NOBODY DOES ANYTHING AROUND HERE BUT ME! — EVERYBODY JUST DROPS THEIR STUFF FOR ME TO PICK UP!
BEER

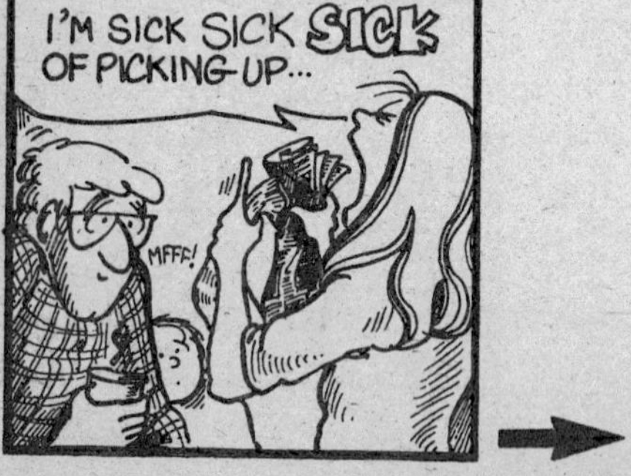
I'M SICK SICK SICK OF PICKING UP...
MFFF!

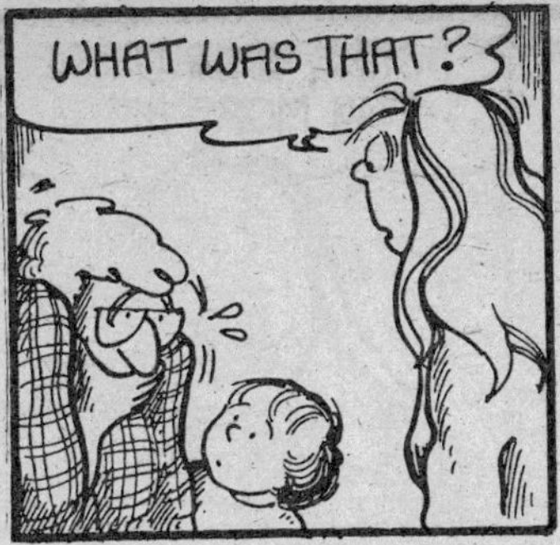
WHAT WAS THAT?

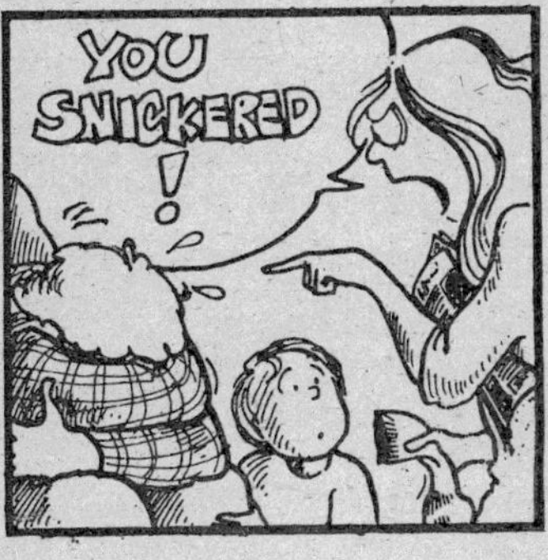
YOU SNICKERED!

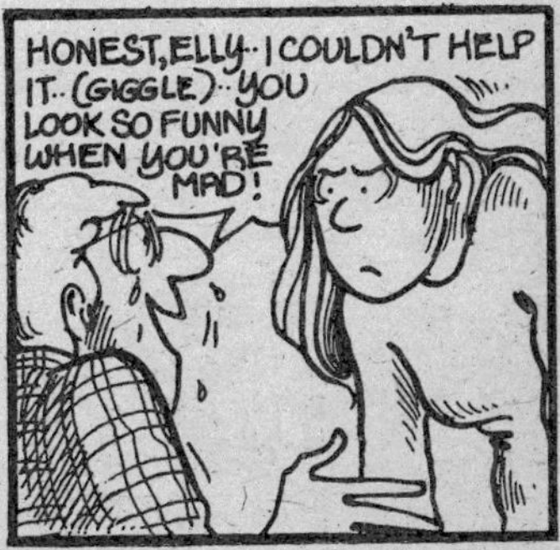
HONEST, ELLY.. I COULDN'T HELP IT.. (GIGGLE).. YOU LOOK SO FUNNY WHEN YOU'RE MAD!

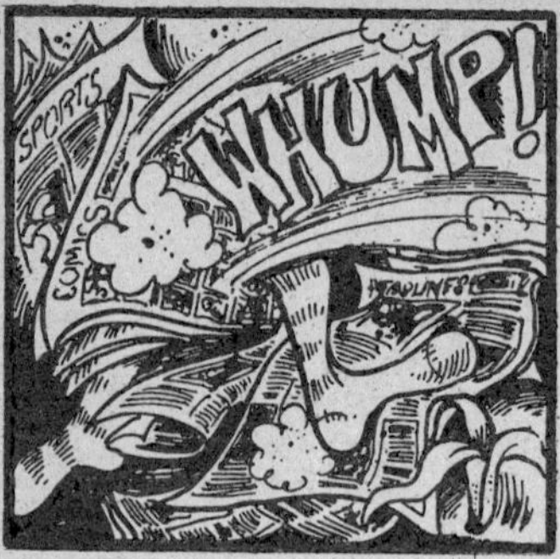
SPORTS
COMICS
WHUMP!

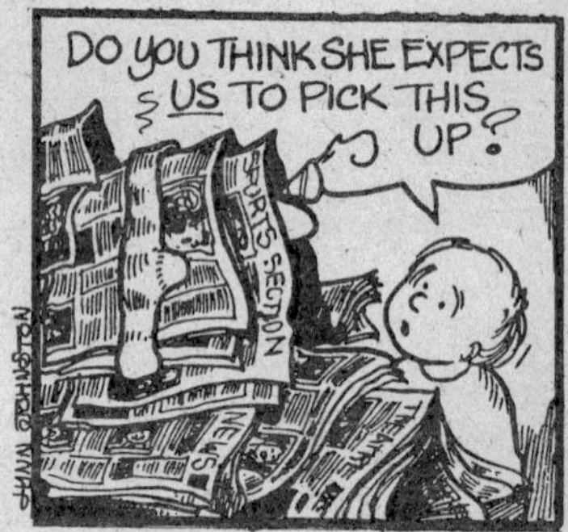
DO YOU THINK SHE EXPECTS US TO PICK THIS UP?
SPORTS SECTION
NEWS
THEATRE

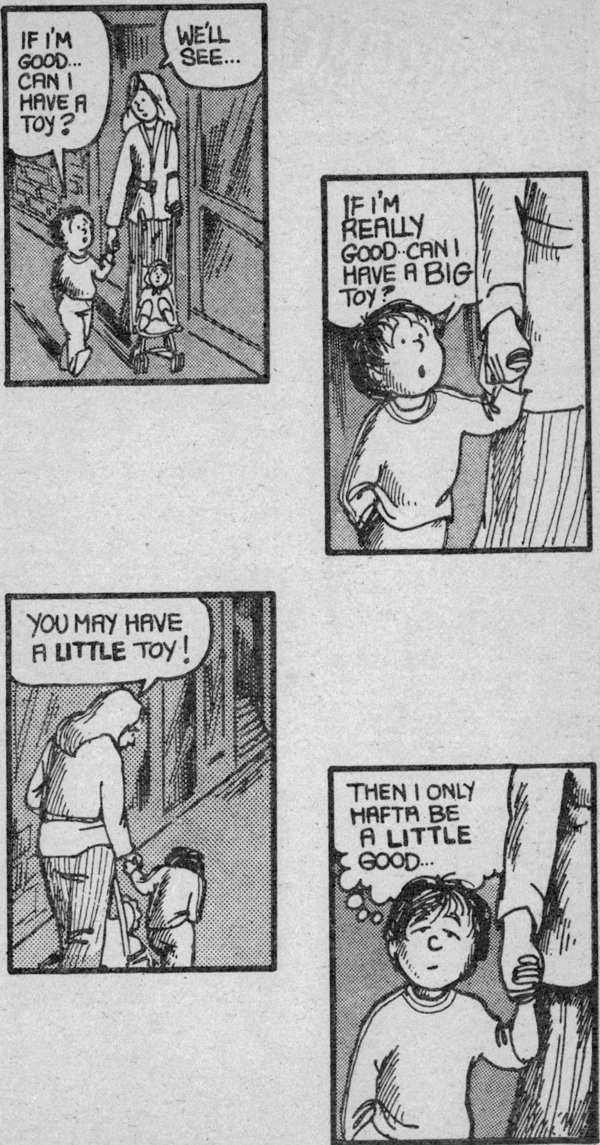
IF I'M GOOD... CAN I HAVE A TOY?
WE'LL SEE...
IF I'M REALLY GOOD..CAN I HAVE A BIG TOY?
YOU MAY HAVE A LITTLE TOY!
THEN I ONLY HAFTA BE A LITTLE GOOD...

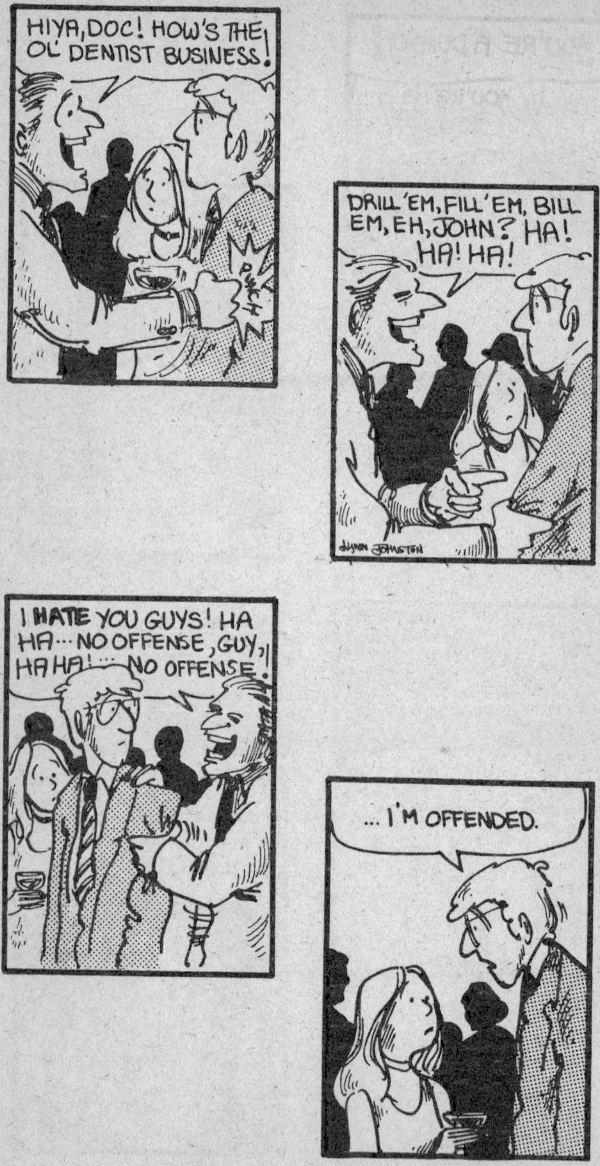
HIYA, DOC! HOW'S THE OL' DENTIST BUSINESS!
PUNCH
DRILL 'EM, FILL 'EM, BILL EM, EH, JOHN? HA! HA! HA!
LYNN JOHNSTON
I HATE YOU GUYS! HA HA... NO OFFENSE, GUY, HA HA!... NO OFFENSE!
... I'M OFFENDED.

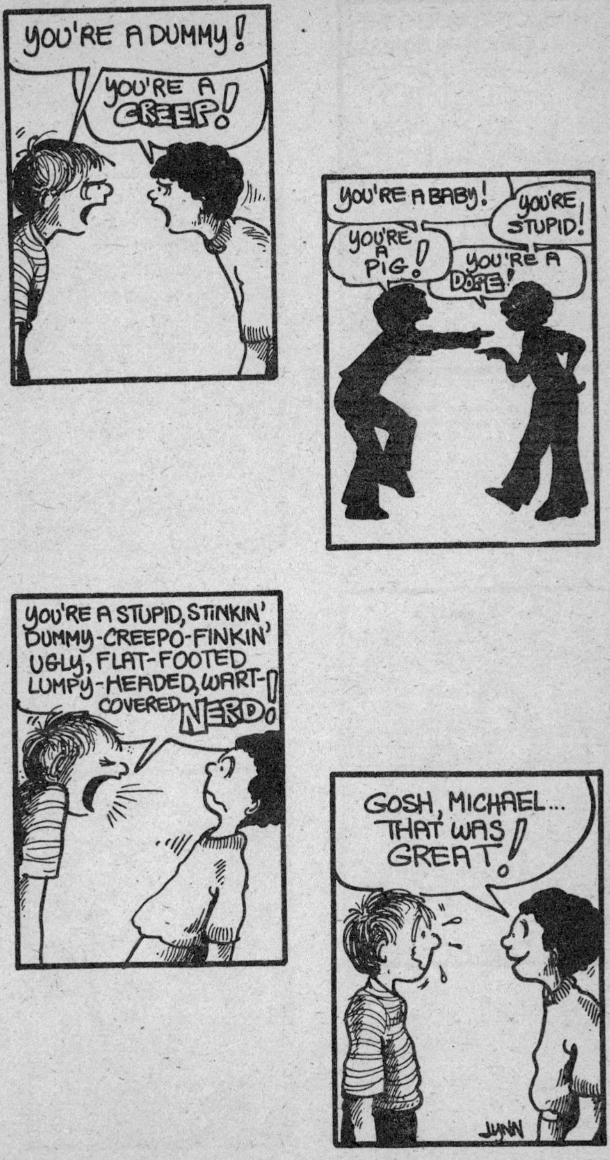
YOU'RE A DUMMY!
YOU'RE A CREEP!
YOU'RE A BABY!
YOU'RE STUPID!
YOU'RE A PIG!
YOU'RE A DOPE!
YOU'RE A STUPID, STINKIN' DUMMY-CREEPO-FINKIN' UGLY, FLAT-FOOTED LUMPY-HEADED, WART-COVERED NERD!
GOSH, MICHAEL... THAT WAS GREAT!
LYNN

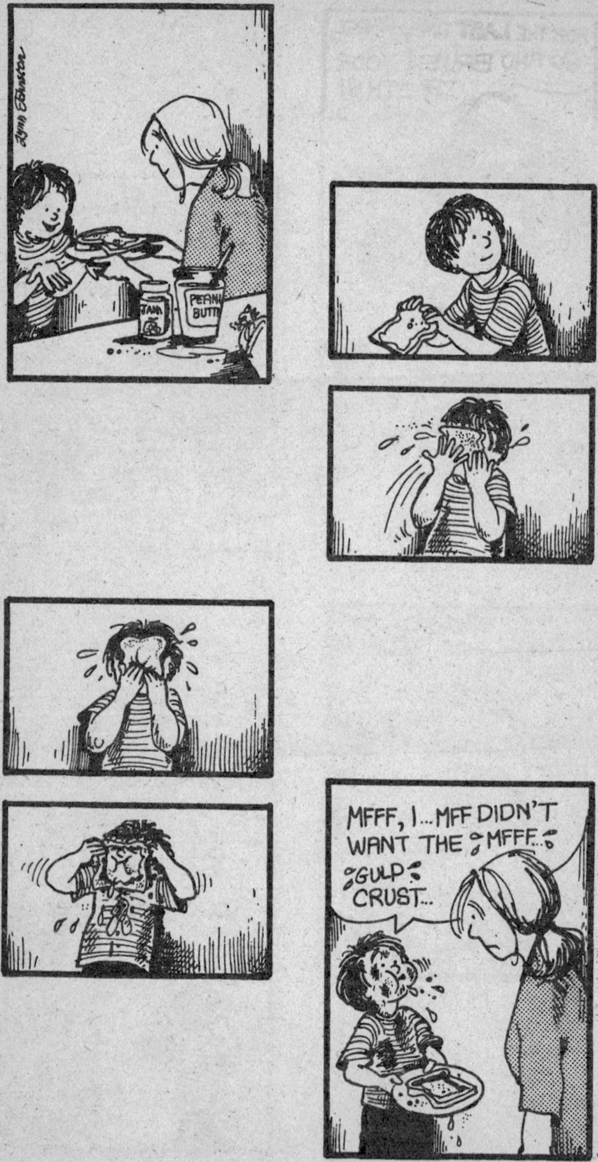
Lynn Johnston
JAM
MFFF, I...MFF DIDN'T WANT THE MFFF... GULP CRUST...

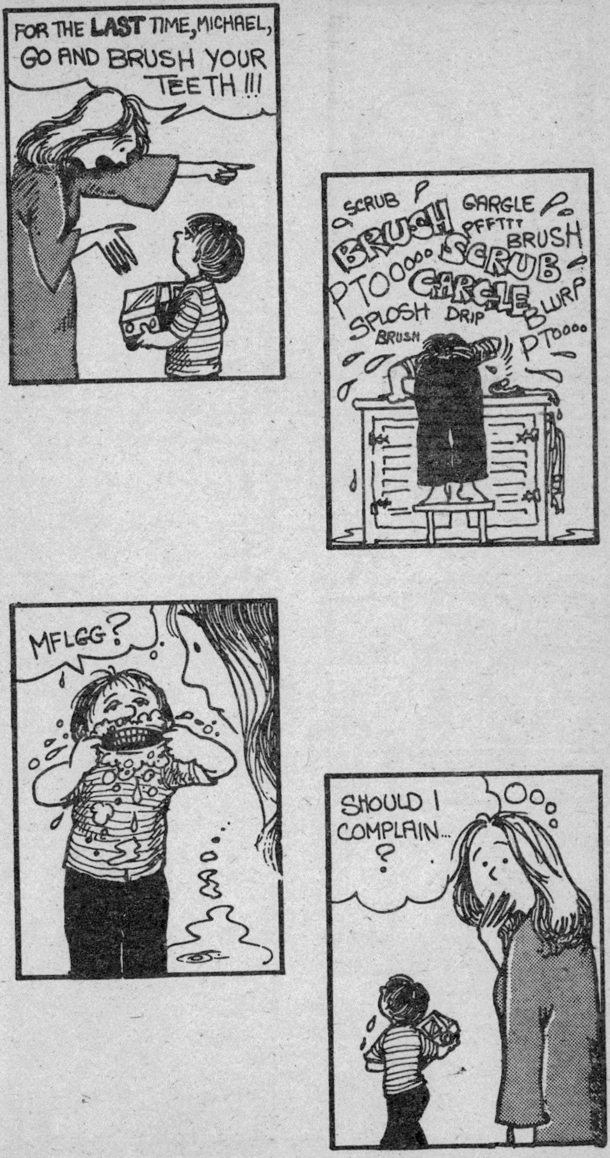
FOR THE **LAST** TIME, MICHAEL, GO AND BRUSH YOUR TEETH !!!
SCRUB
GARGLE
BRUSH
PFFTTT
BRUSH
PTOOooo
SCRUB
GARGLE
SPLOSH
DRIP
BLURP
BRUSH
PTOooo
MFLGG?
SHOULD I COMPLAIN... ?

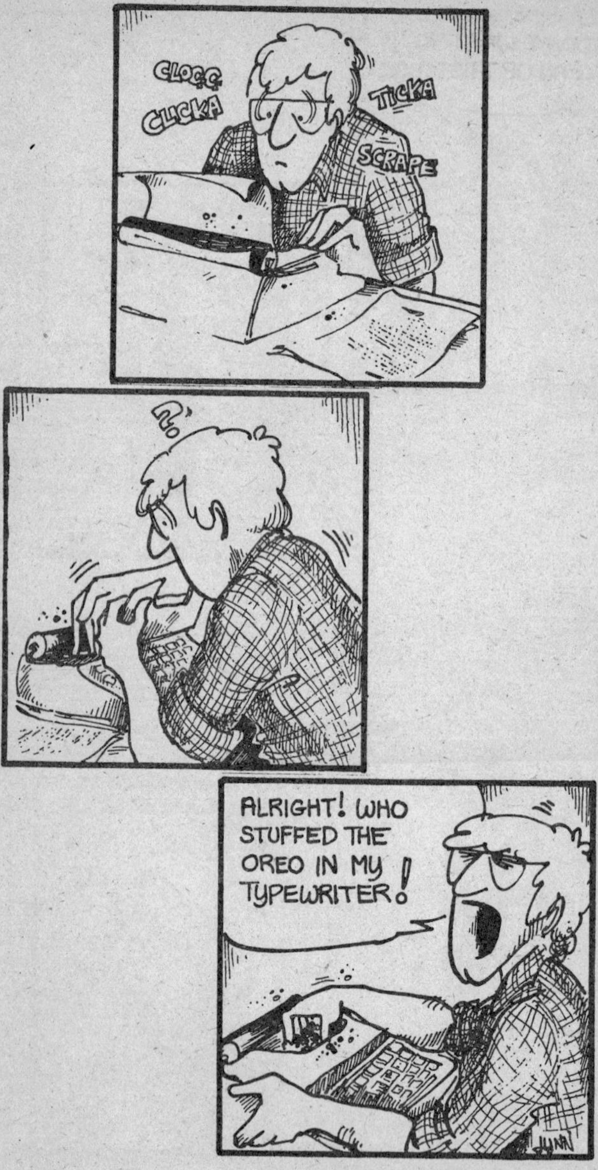
CLOGG
CLICKA
TICKA
SCRAPE
?
ALRIGHT! WHO STUFFED THE OREO IN MY TYPEWRITER!

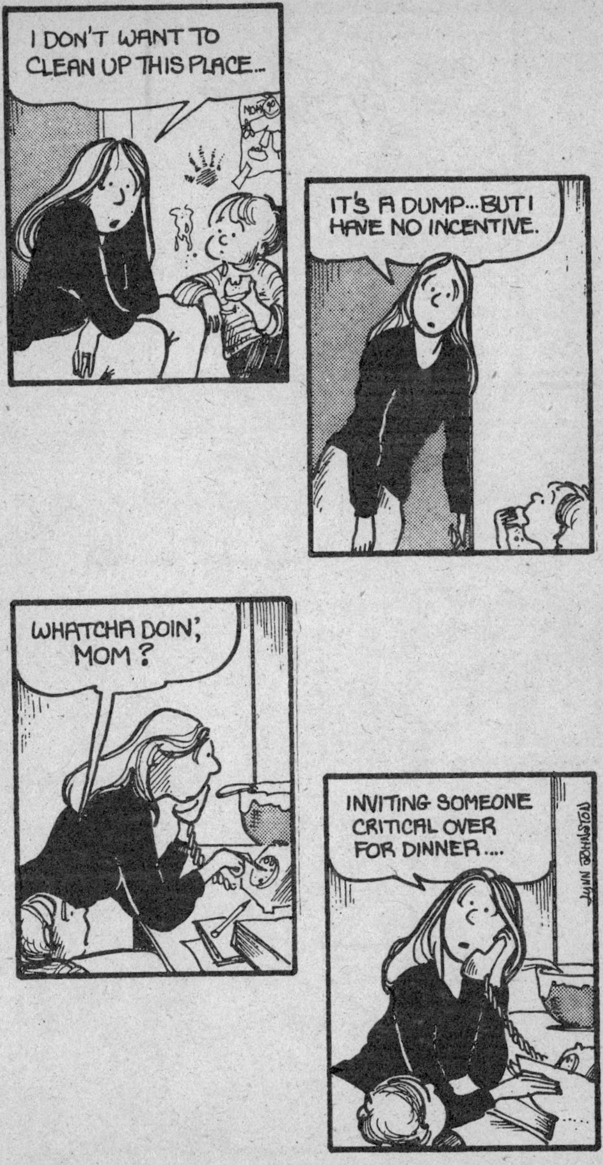
I DON'T WANT TO CLEAN UP THIS PLACE...
IT'S A DUMP...BUT I HAVE NO INCENTIVE.
WHATCHA DOIN', MOM?
INVITING SOMEONE CRITICAL OVER FOR DINNER....
LYNN JOHNSTON

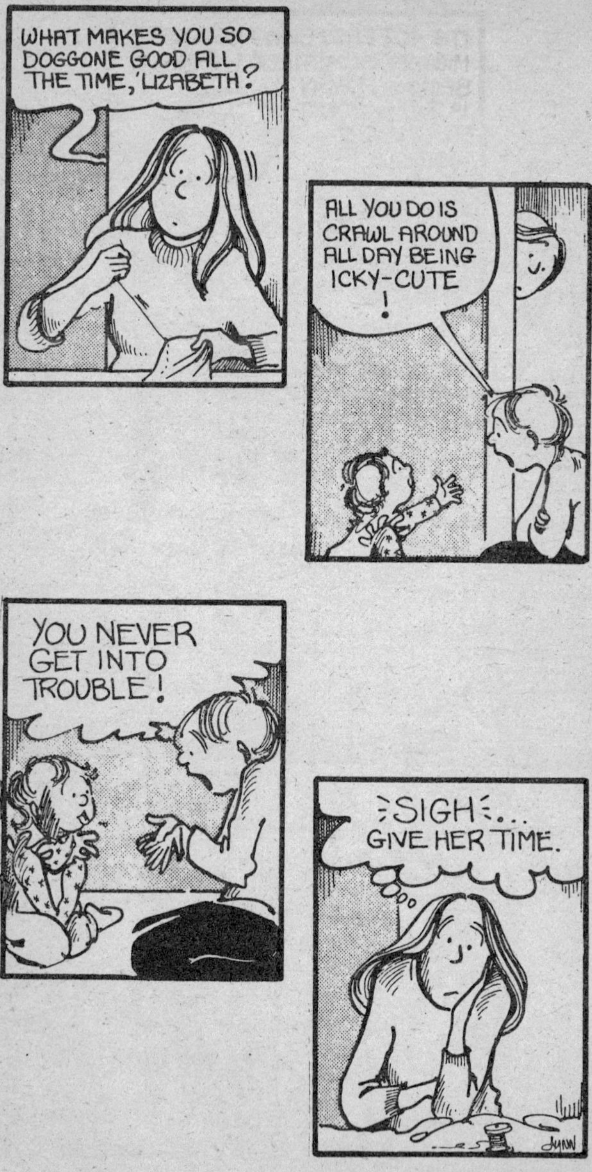
WHAT MAKES YOU SO DOGGONE GOOD ALL THE TIME, 'LIZABETH?
ALL YOU DO IS CRAWL AROUND ALL DAY BEING ICKY-CUTE!
YOU NEVER GET INTO TROUBLE!
SIGH... GIVE HER TIME.

IT'S NOT EASY BEING A GROWNUP, MICHAEL. SOMETIMES I THINK BEING A MOMMY IS THE HARDEST THING IN THE WORLD...
I DON'T LIKE GETTING ANGRY. I FEEL BAD WHEN I HAVE TO PUNISH YOU. ARE YOU LISTENING, HONEY?
YEAH. HOWCOME A NOSE HAS ONLY TWO HOLES IN IT?

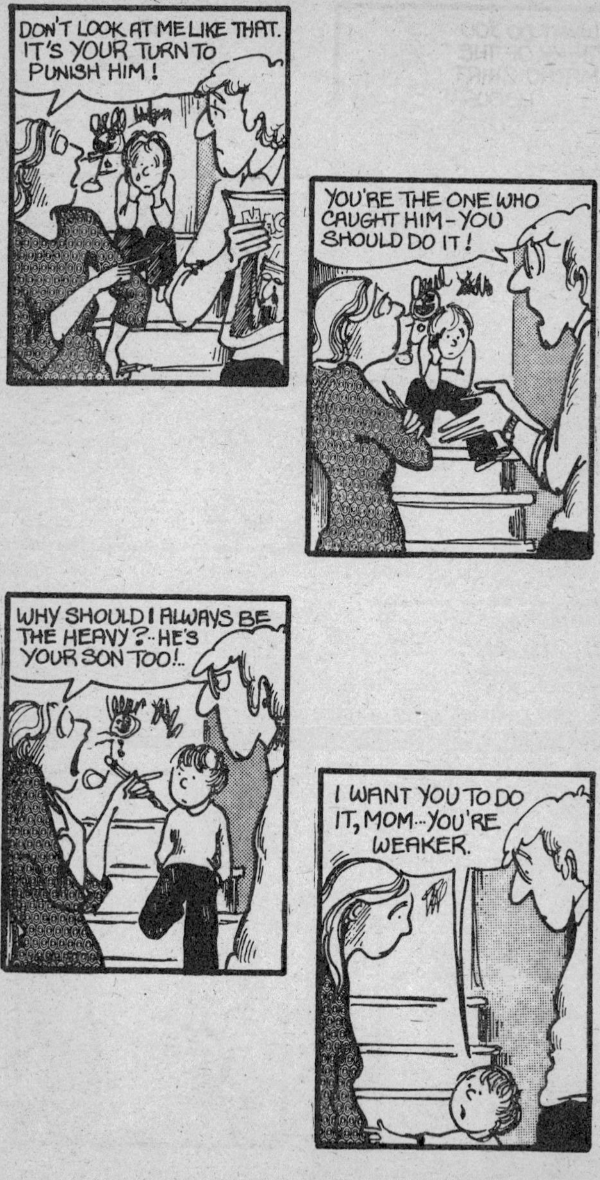
DON'T LOOK AT ME LIKE THAT. IT'S YOUR TURN TO PUNISH HIM!
YOU'RE THE ONE WHO CAUGHT HIM - YOU SHOULD DO IT!
WHY SHOULD I ALWAYS BE THE HEAVY?.. HE'S YOUR SON TOO!..
I WANT YOU TO DO IT, MOM... YOU'RE WEAKER.

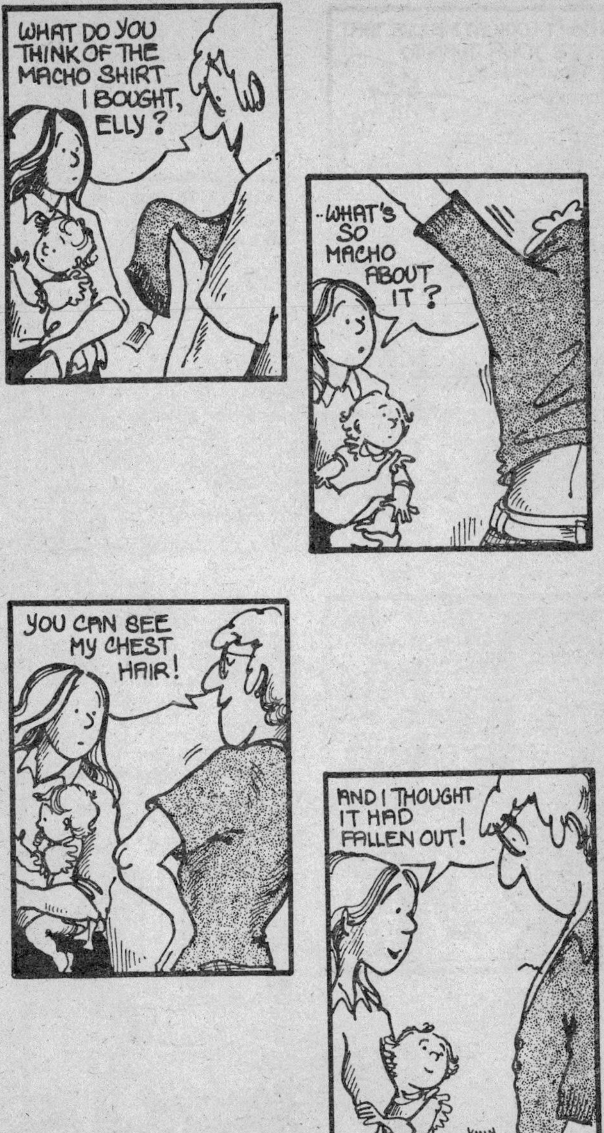
WHAT DO YOU THINK OF THE MACHO SHIRT I BOUGHT, ELLY?
..WHAT'S SO MACHO ABOUT IT?
YOU CAN SEE MY CHEST HAIR!
AND I THOUGHT IT HAD FALLEN OUT!
Lynn

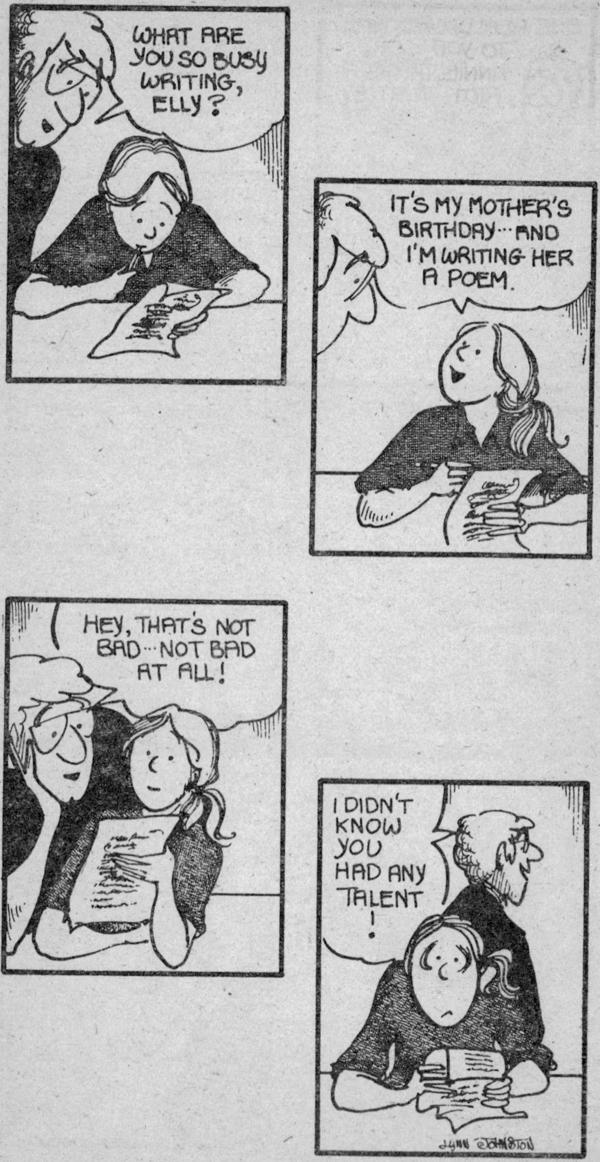
WHAT ARE YOU SO BUSY WRITING, ELLY?
IT'S MY MOTHER'S BIRTHDAY... AND I'M WRITING HER A POEM.
HEY, THAT'S NOT BAD... NOT BAD AT ALL!
I DIDN'T KNOW YOU HAD ANY TALENT!
LYNN JOHNSTON

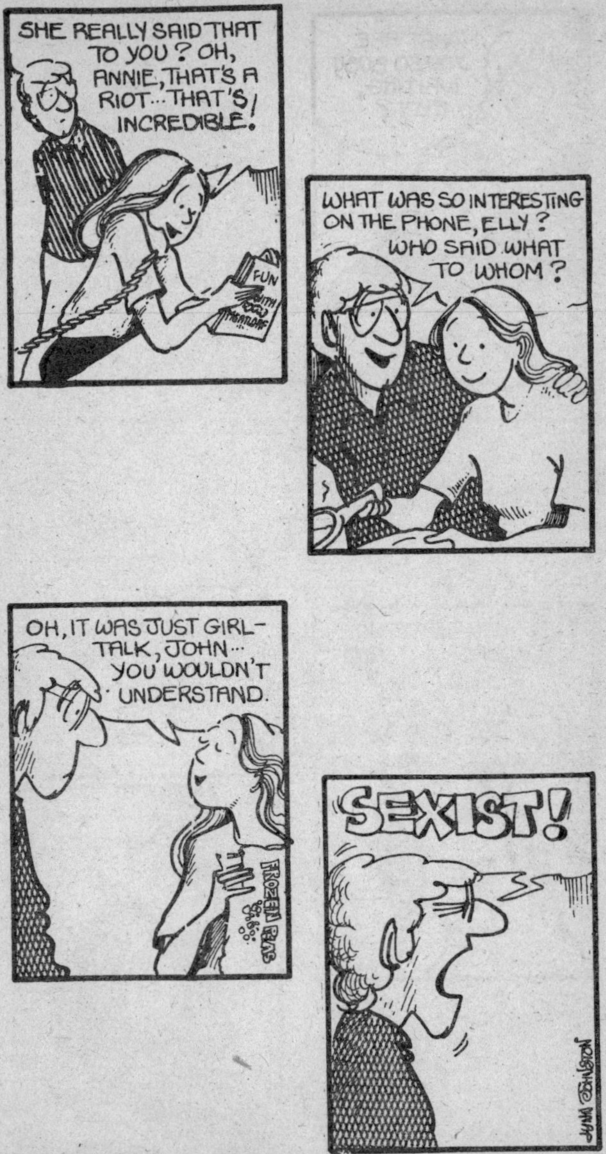
SHE REALLY SAID THAT TO YOU? OH, ANNIE, THAT'S A RIOT... THAT'S INCREDIBLE!
FUN
WHAT WAS SO INTERESTING ON THE PHONE, ELLY? WHO SAID WHAT TO WHOM?
OH, IT WAS JUST GIRL-TALK, JOHN... YOU WOULDN'T UNDERSTAND.
FROZEN PEAS
SEXIST!
LYNN JOHNSTON

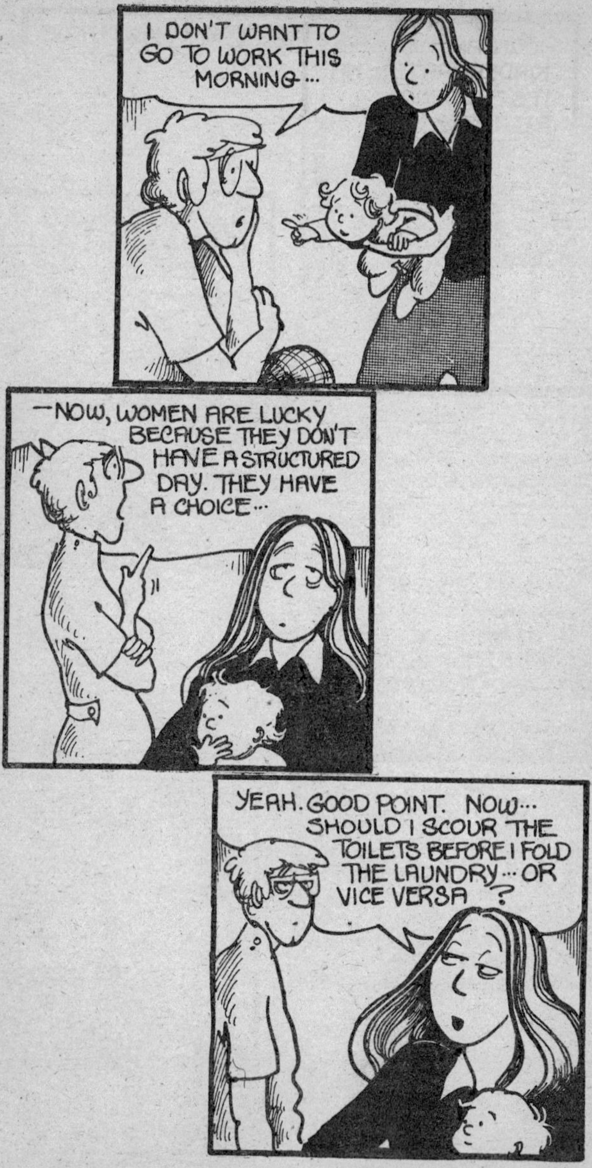
I DON'T WANT TO GO TO WORK THIS MORNING...
—NOW, WOMEN ARE LUCKY BECAUSE THEY DON'T HAVE A STRUCTURED DAY. THEY HAVE A CHOICE...
YEAH. GOOD POINT. NOW... SHOULD I SCOUR THE TOILETS BEFORE I FOLD THE LAUNDRY... OR VICE VERSA ?

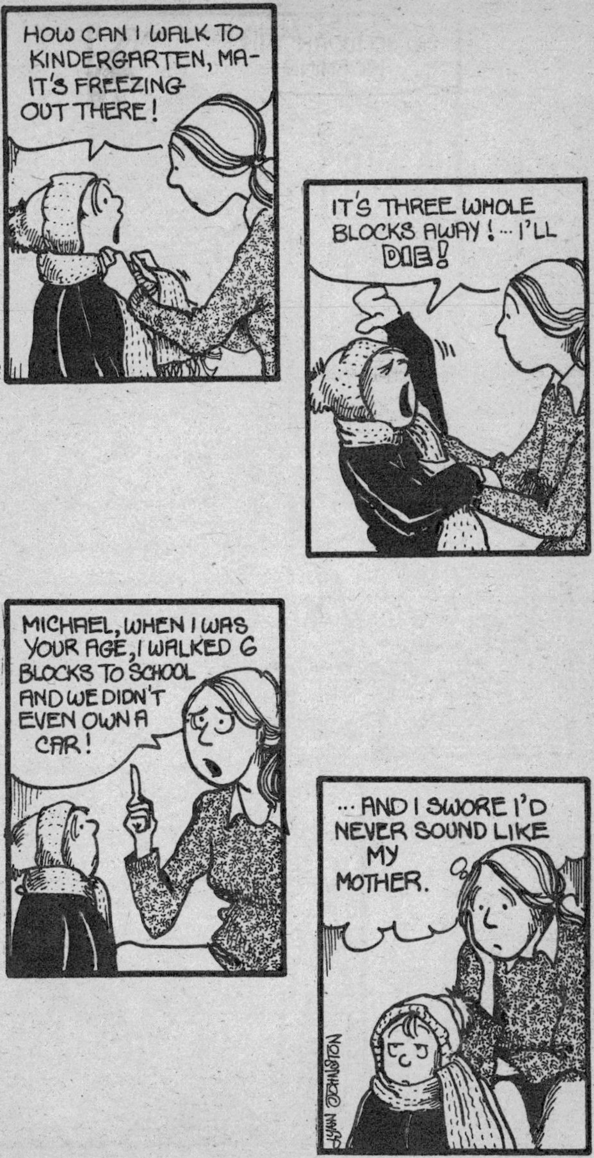
HOW CAN I WALK TO KINDERGARTEN, MA- IT'S FREEZING OUT THERE!
IT'S THREE WHOLE BLOCKS AWAY! ... I'LL DIE!
MICHAEL, WHEN I WAS YOUR AGE, I WALKED 6 BLOCKS TO SCHOOL AND WE DIDN'T EVEN OWN A CAR!
... AND I SWORE I'D NEVER SOUND LIKE MY MOTHER.
LYNN JOHNSTON

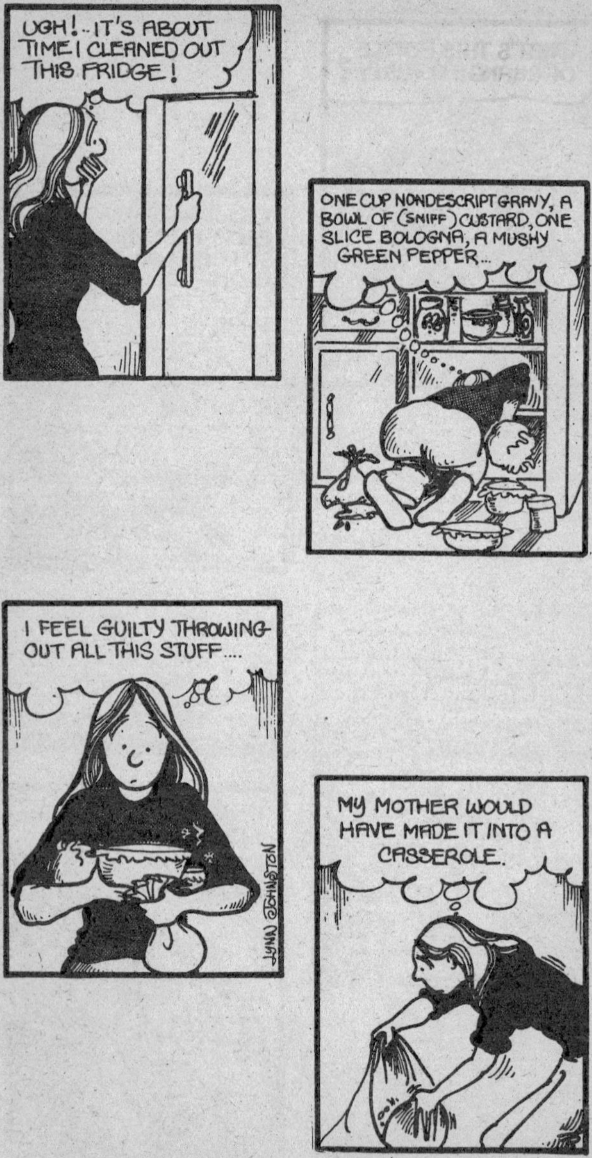
UGH!..IT'S ABOUT TIME I CLEANED OUT THIS FRIDGE!
ONE CUP NONDESCRIPT GRAVY, A BOWL OF (SNIFF) CUSTARD, ONE SLICE BOLOGNA, A MUSHY GREEN PEPPER...
I FEEL GUILTY THROWING OUT ALL THIS STUFF....
LYNN JOHNSTON
MY MOTHER WOULD HAVE MADE IT INTO A CASSEROLE.

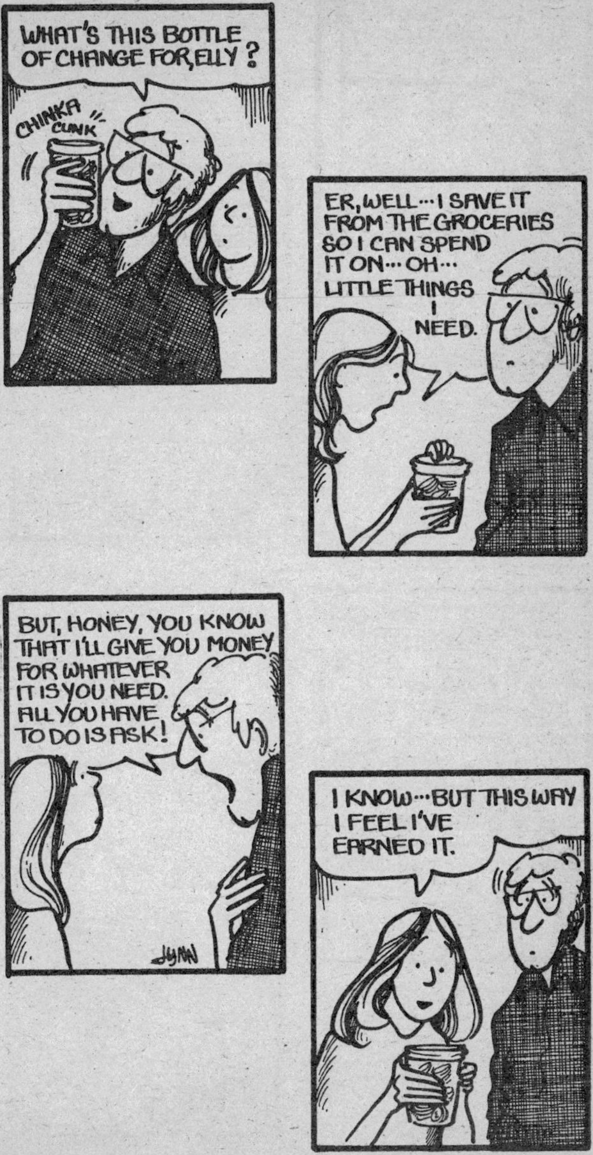
WHAT'S THIS BOTTLE OF CHANGE FOR, ELLY?
CHINKA CLINK
ER, WELL... I SAVE IT FROM THE GROCERIES SO I CAN SPEND IT ON... OH... LITTLE THINGS I NEED.
BUT, HONEY, YOU KNOW THAT I'LL GIVE YOU MONEY FOR WHATEVER IT IS YOU NEED. ALL YOU HAVE TO DO IS ASK!
I KNOW... BUT THIS WAY I FEEL I'VE EARNED IT.

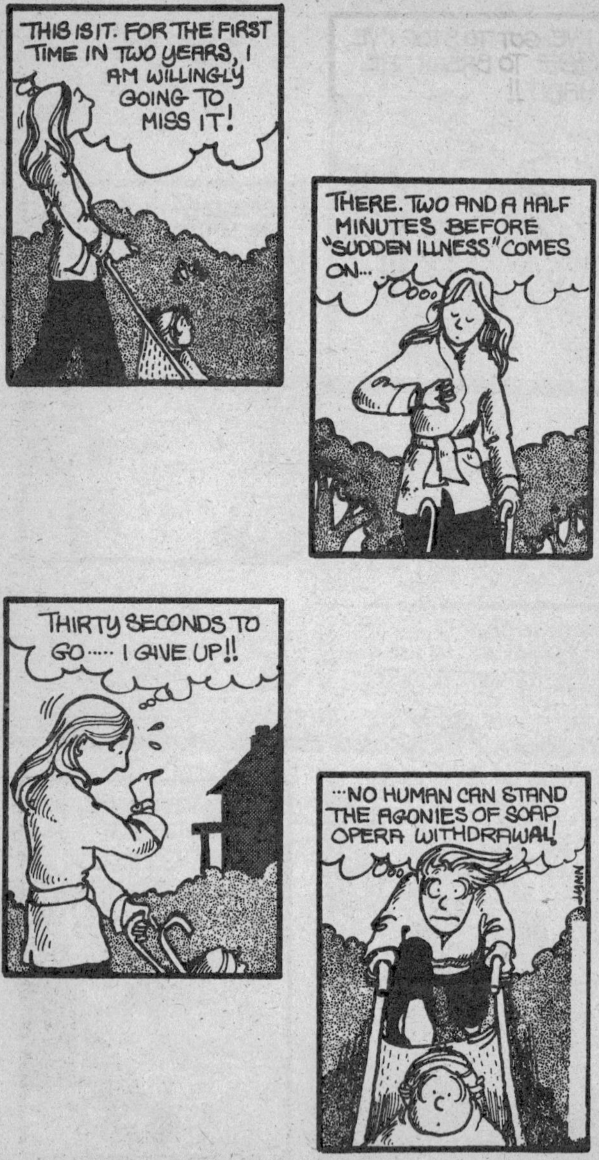
THIS IS IT. FOR THE FIRST TIME IN TWO YEARS, I AM WILLINGLY GOING TO MISS IT!
THERE. TWO AND A HALF MINUTES BEFORE "SUDDEN ILLNESS" COMES ON...
THIRTY SECONDS TO GO..... I GIVE UP!!
...NO HUMAN CAN STAND THE AGONIES OF SOAP OPERA WITHDRAWAL!

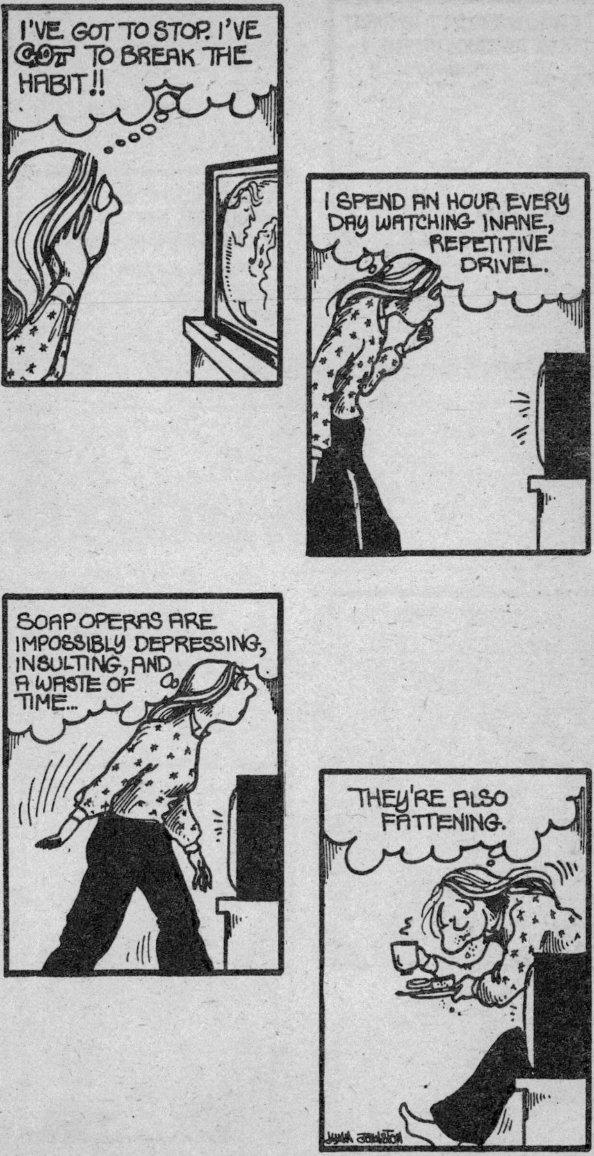

I'VE GOT TO STOP. I'VE GOT TO BREAK THE HABIT!!
I SPEND AN HOUR EVERY DAY WATCHING INANE, REPETITIVE DRIVEL.
SOAP OPERAS ARE IMPOSSIBLY DEPRESSING, INSULTING, AND A WASTE OF TIME...
THEY'RE ALSO FATTENING.

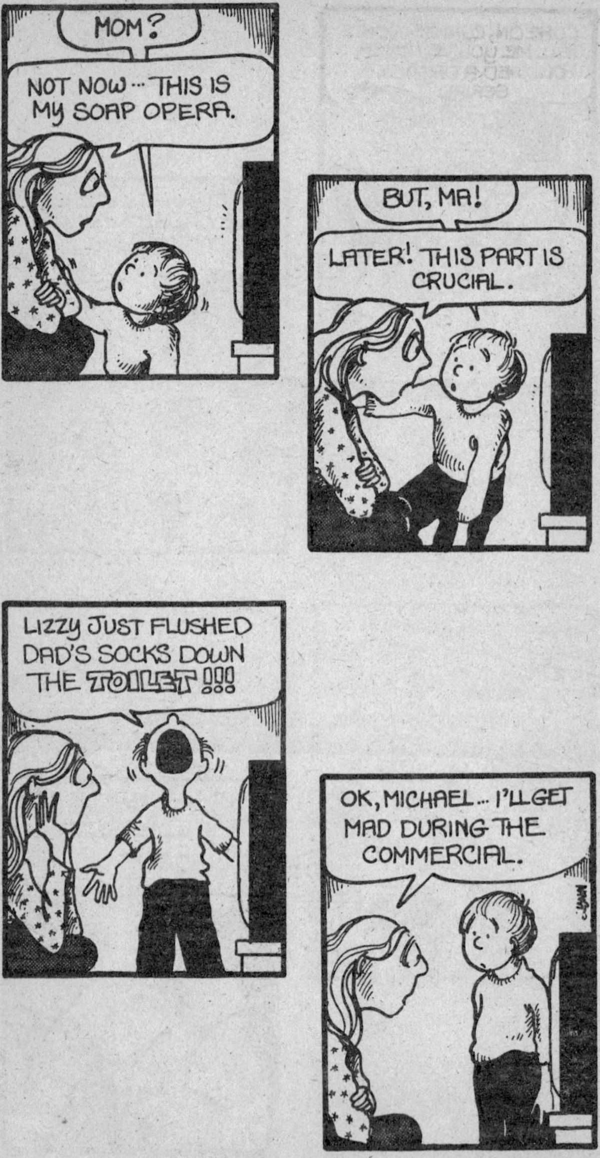
MOM?
NOT NOW... THIS IS MY SOAP OPERA.
BUT, MA!
LATER! THIS PART IS CRUCIAL.
LIZZY JUST FLUSHED DAD'S SOCKS DOWN THE TOILET!!!
OK, MICHAEL... I'LL GET MAD DURING THE COMMERCIAL.

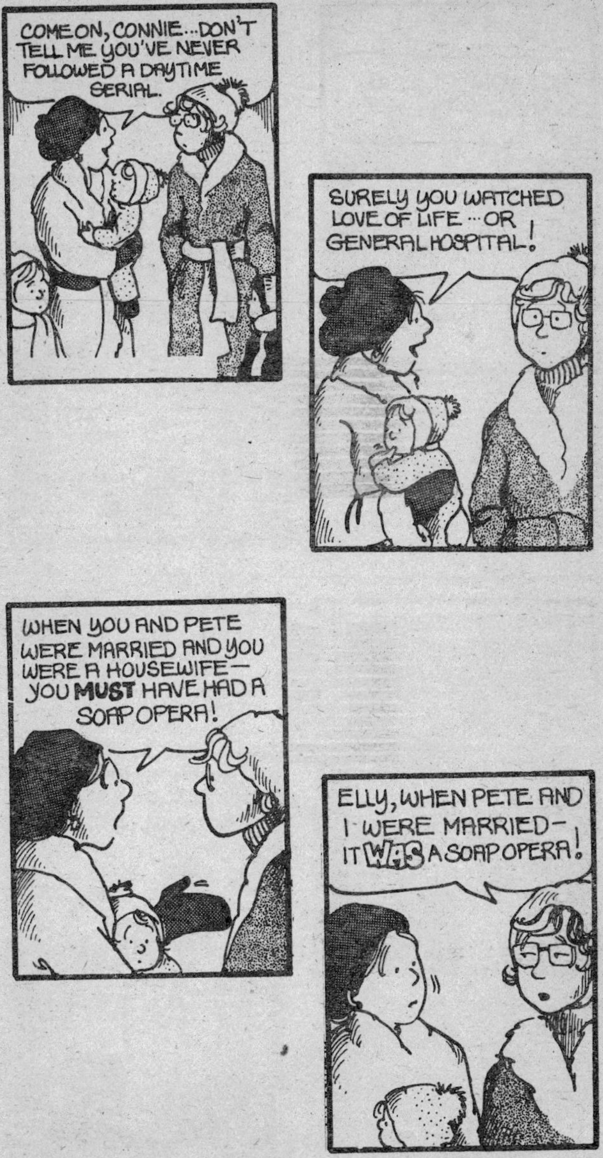
COME ON, CONNIE...DON'T TELL ME YOU'VE NEVER FOLLOWED A DAYTIME SERIAL.
SURELY YOU WATCHED LOVE OF LIFE ...OR GENERAL HOSPITAL!
WHEN YOU AND PETE WERE MARRIED AND YOU WERE A HOUSEWIFE— YOU MUST HAVE HAD A SOAP OPERA!
ELLY, WHEN PETE AND I WERE MARRIED— IT WAS A SOAP OPERA!

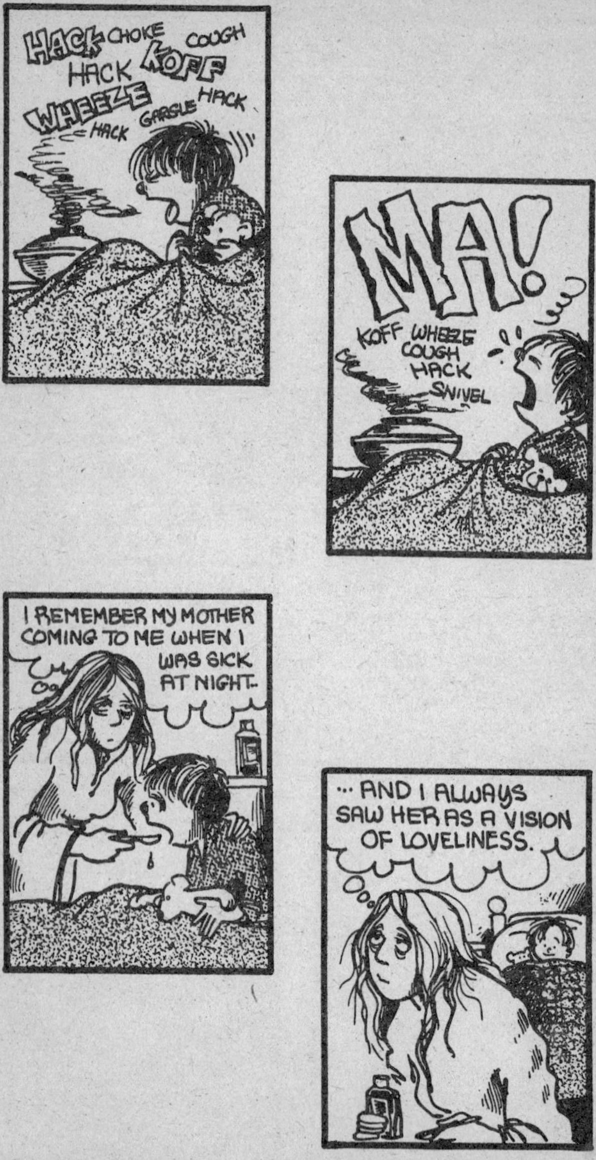
HACK CHOKE COUGH
HACK KOFF
WHEEZE HACK
GARGLE
HACK
MA!
KOFF WHEEZE
COUGH
HACK
SNIVEL
I REMEMBER MY MOTHER COMING TO ME WHEN I WAS SICK AT NIGHT.
... AND I ALWAYS SAW HER AS A VISION OF LOVELINESS.